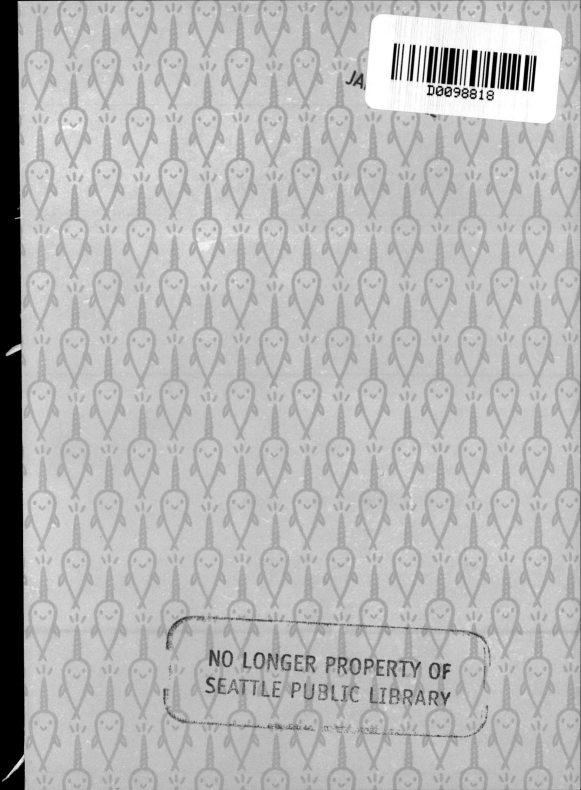

# HAVE YOU READ THESE
# NARWHAL AND JELLY BOOKS?

SUPER NARWHAL AND JELLY JOLT

PEANUT BUTTER AND JELLY

# NARWHAL

## UNICORN OF THE SEA

# BEN CLANTON

tundra

# FOR ENYA
## A.K.A. NUNU, A.K.A. JELLYFISH-FLINGER,
## A.K.A. MERMICORN

Text and illustrations copyright © 2016 by Ben Clanton

Tundra Books, an imprint of Penguin Random House Canada Young Readers, a Penguin Random House Company

Library and Archives Canada Cataloguing in Publication

Clanton, Ben, 1988-, author, illustrator
Narwhal : unicorn of the sea / written and illustrated
by Ben Clanton.

Issued in print and electronic formats.
ISBN 978-1-101-91826-5 (bound).–ISBN 978-1-101-91871-5 (paperback)
ISBN 978-1-101-91827-2 (epub)

I. Title.

PZ7.C523Na 2016            j813'.6            C2015-905757-4
                                              C2015-905758-2

Published simultaneously in the United States of America by Tundra Books of Northern New York, an imprint of Penguin Random House Canada Young Readers, a Penguin Random House Company

Library of Congress Control Number: 2015955122

Edited by Tara Walker
Designed by Ben Clanton and Andrew Roberts
The artwork in this book was rendered in colored pencil and colored digitally.
The text was hand-lettered by Ben Clanton.
Photos: (waffle) © Tiger Images/Shutterstock; (strawberry) © Valentina Razumova/Shutterstock
Printed and bound in China

www.penguinrandomhouse.ca

9   10   11   12      21   20   19   18

Penguin
Random House
TUNDRA BOOKS

# CONTENTS

N

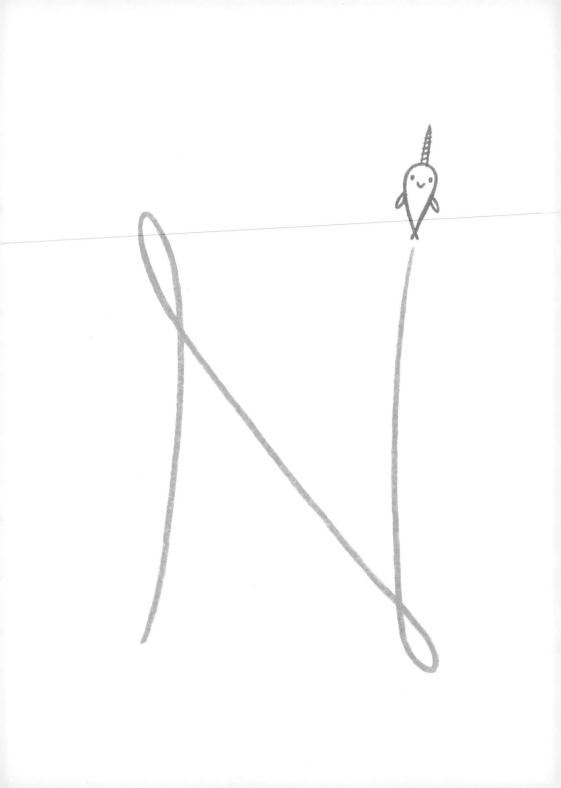

NARWHAL IS REAL~~LY~~ AWESOME

ONE DAY WHEN NARWHAL WAS OUT FOR A SWIM, HE FOUND HIMSELF IN NEW WATERS.

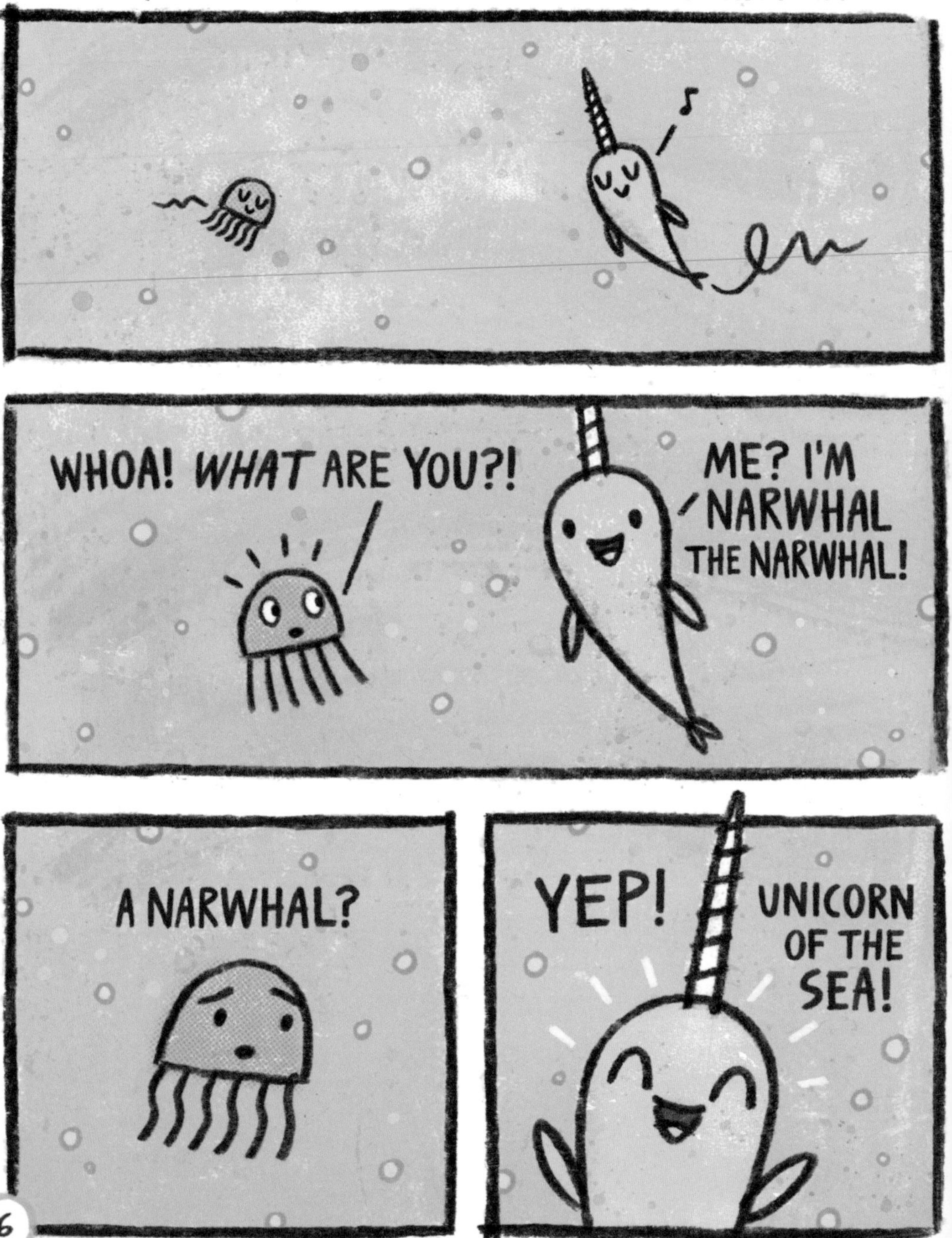
WHOA! *WHAT* ARE YOU?!
ME? I'M NARWHAL THE NARWHAL!
A NARWHAL?
YEP!
UNICORN OF THE SEA!

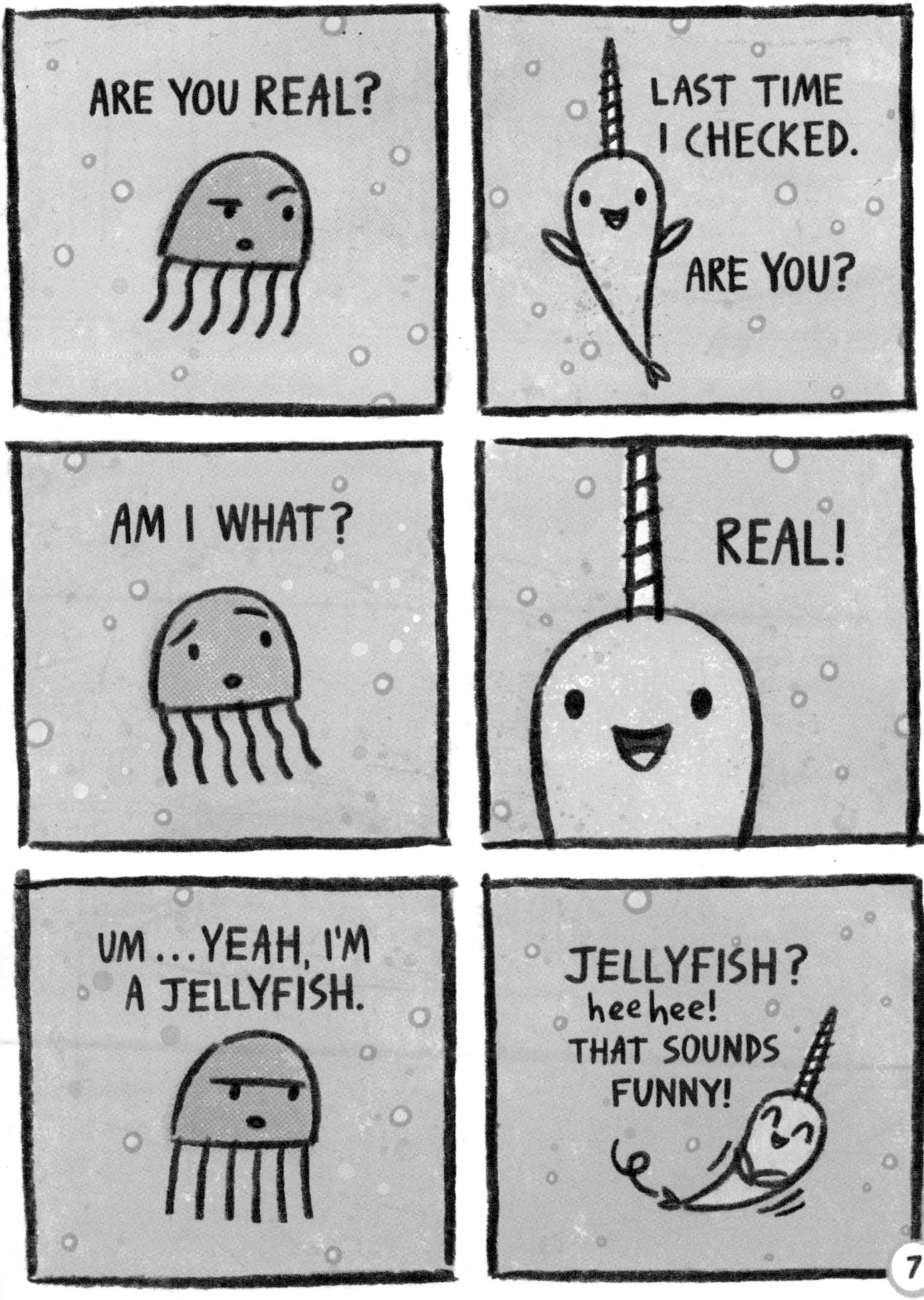
ARE YOU REAL?
LAST TIME I CHECKED.
ARE YOU?
AM I WHAT?
REAL!
UM...YEAH, I'M A JELLYFISH.
JELLYFISH?
heehee!
THAT SOUNDS FUNNY!

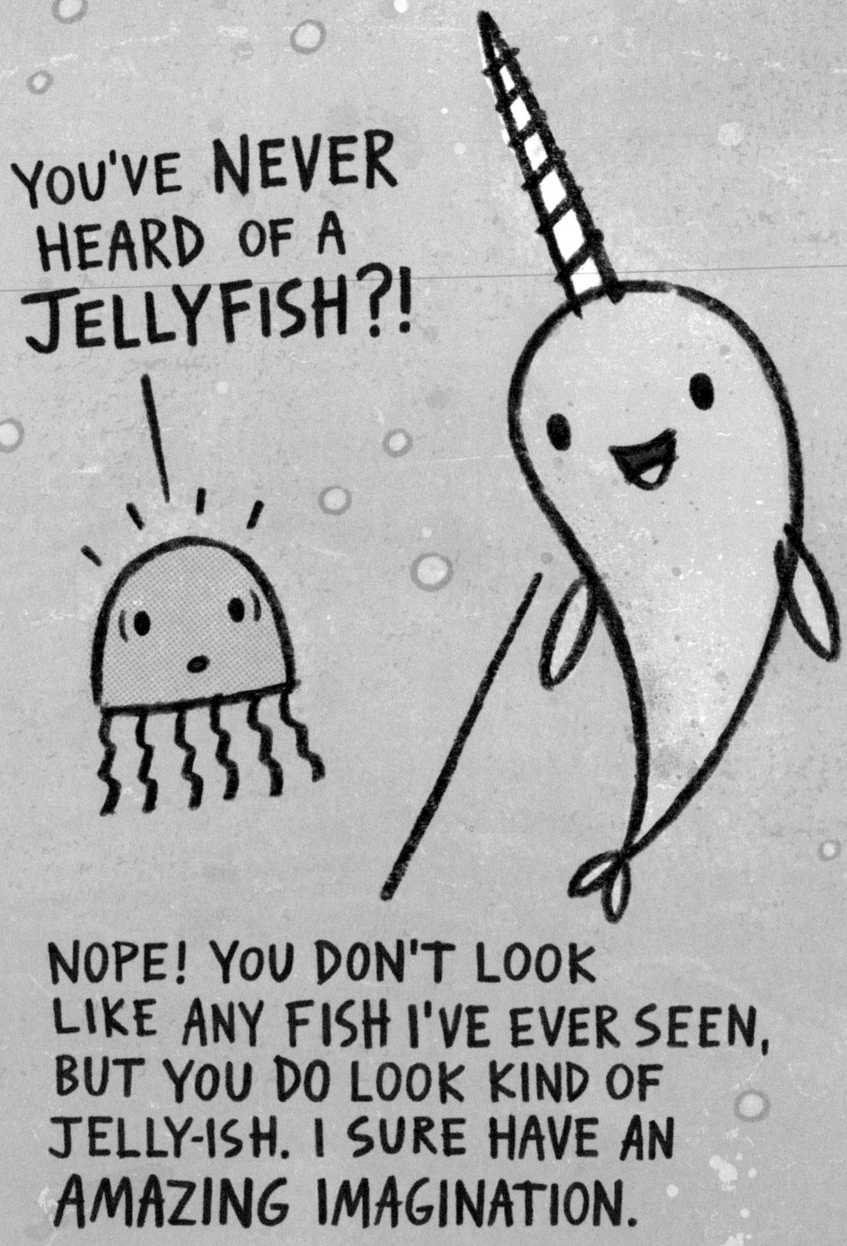
YOU'VE NEVER HEARD OF A JELLYFISH?!
NOPE! YOU DON'T LOOK LIKE ANY FISH I'VE EVER SEEN, BUT YOU DO LOOK KIND OF JELLY-ISH. I SURE HAVE AN AMAZING IMAGINATION.

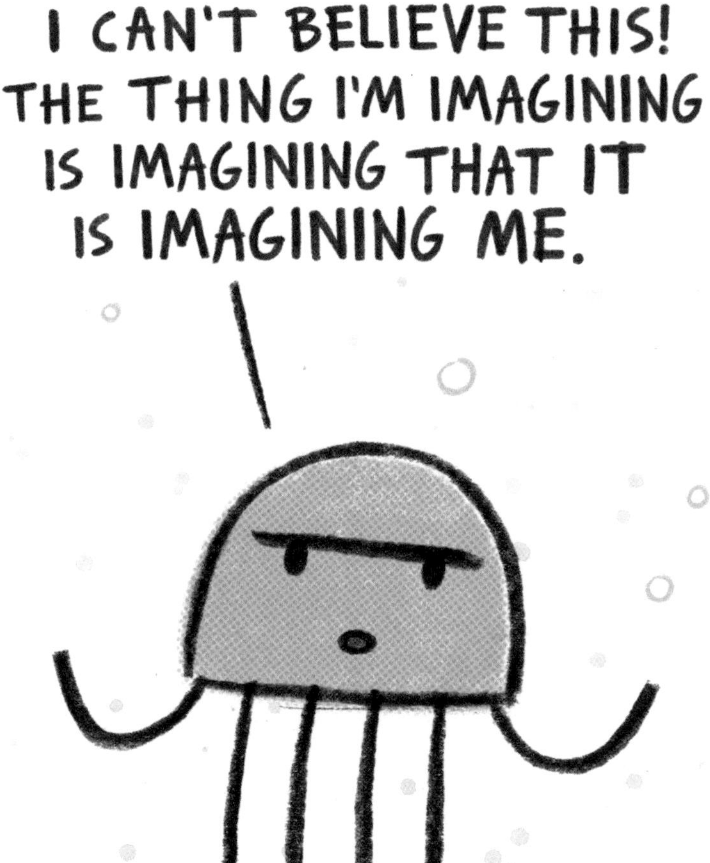
I CAN'T BELIEVE THIS! THE THING I'M IMAGINING IS IMAGINING THAT IT IS IMAGINING ME.

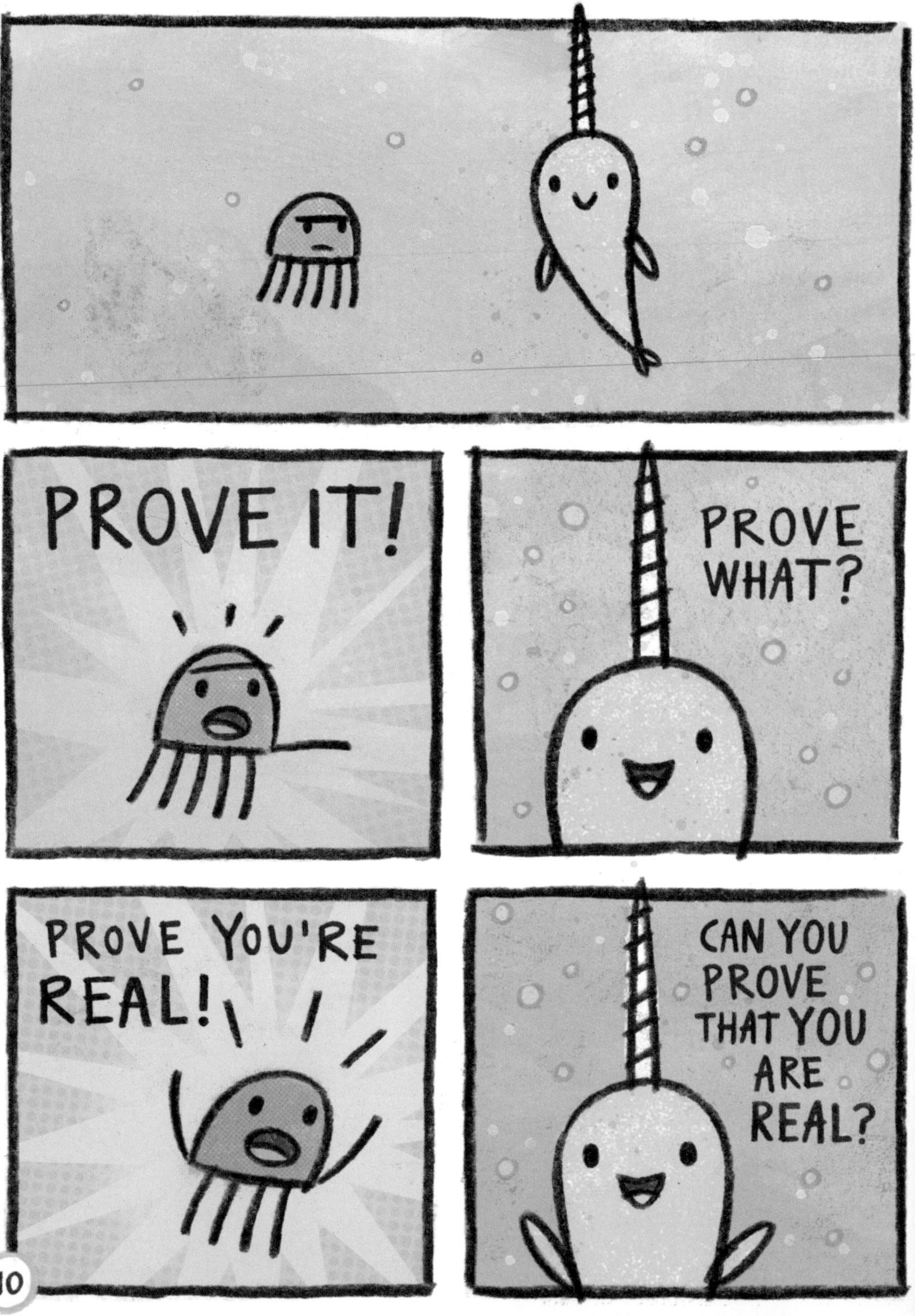
PROVE IT!
PROVE WHAT?
PROVE YOU'RE REAL!
CAN YOU PROVE THAT YOU ARE REAL?

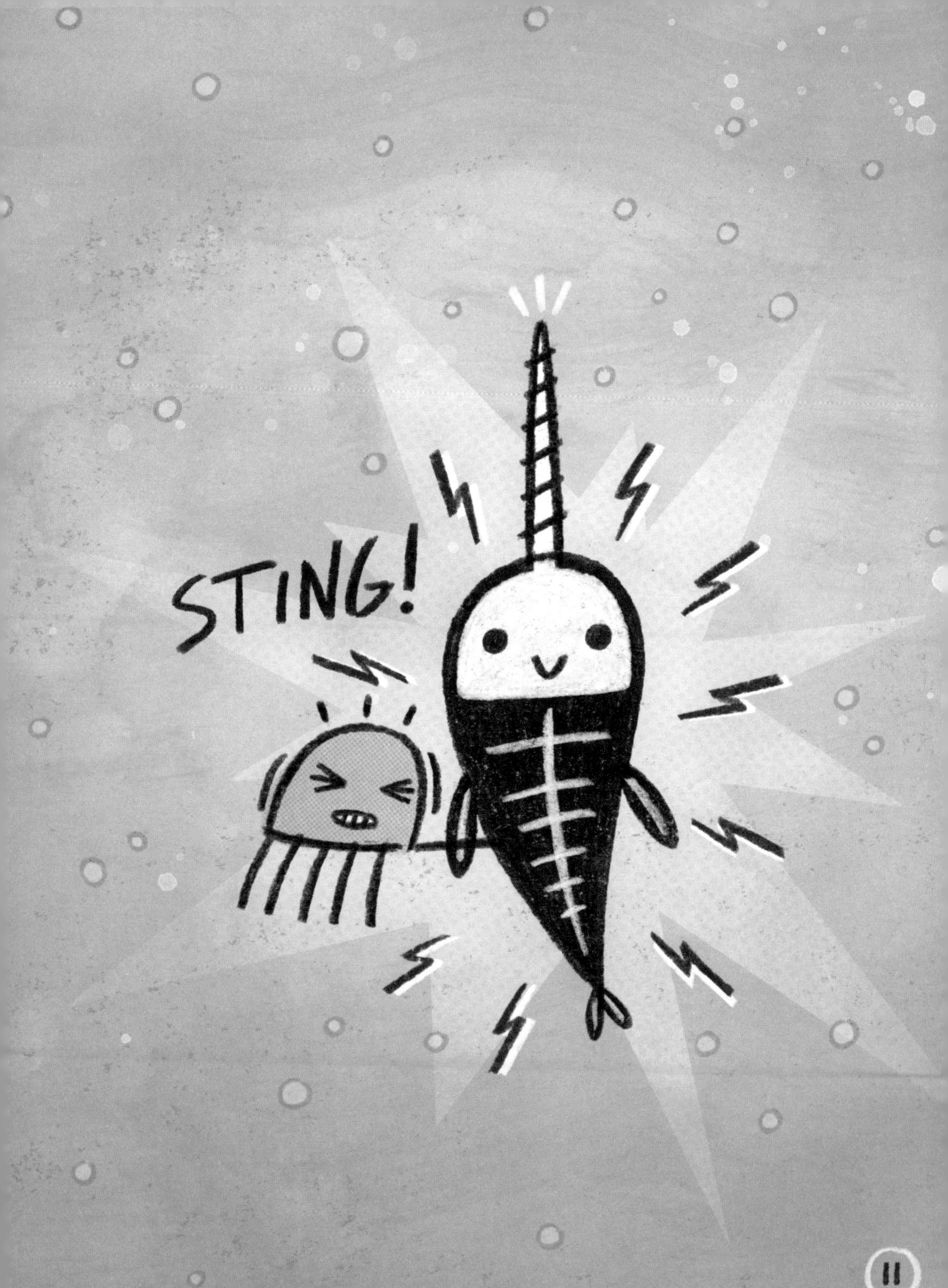
STING!

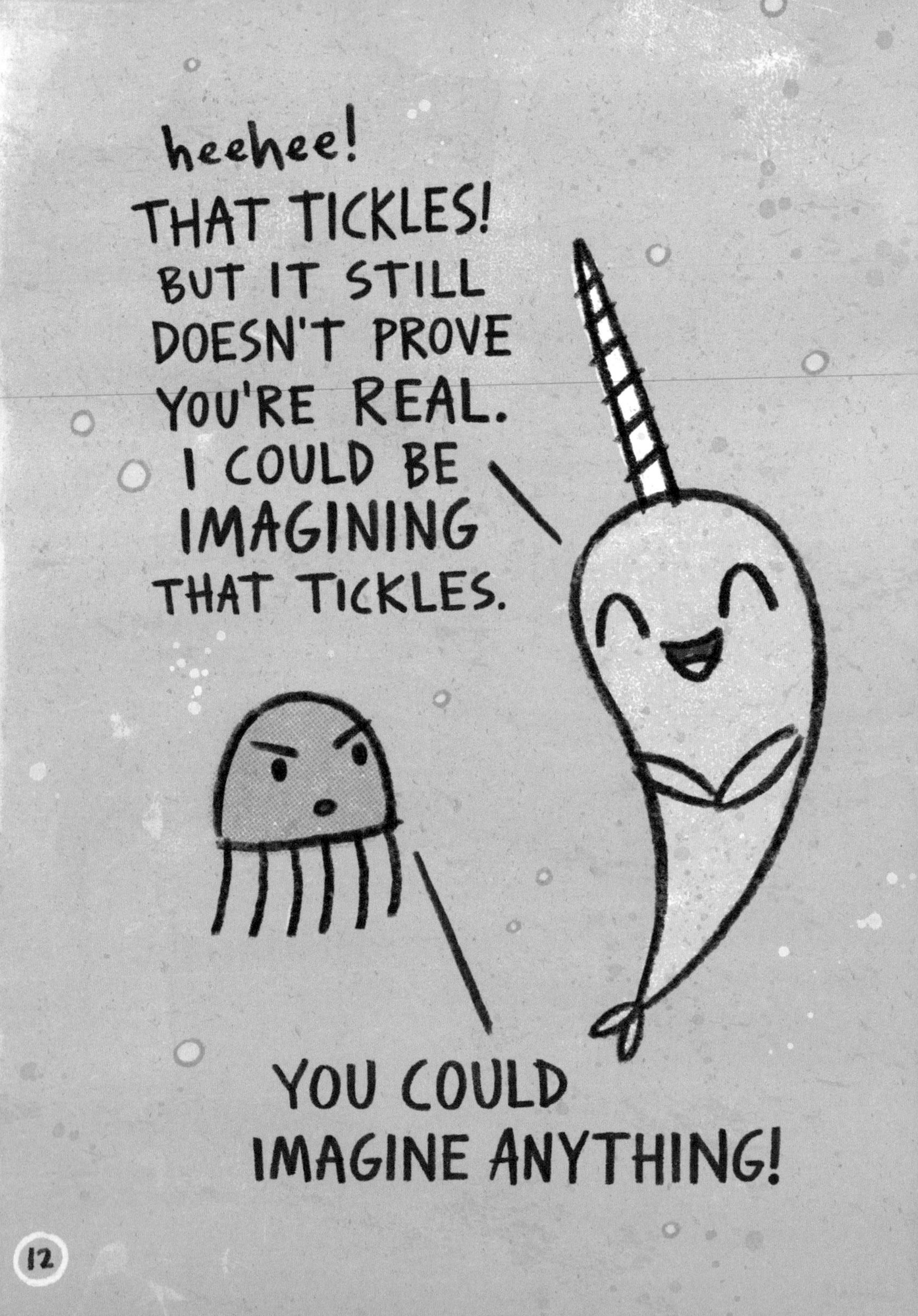
heehee!
THAT TICKLES! BUT IT STILL DOESN'T PROVE YOU'RE REAL. I COULD BE IMAGINING THAT TICKLES.
YOU COULD IMAGINE ANYTHING!

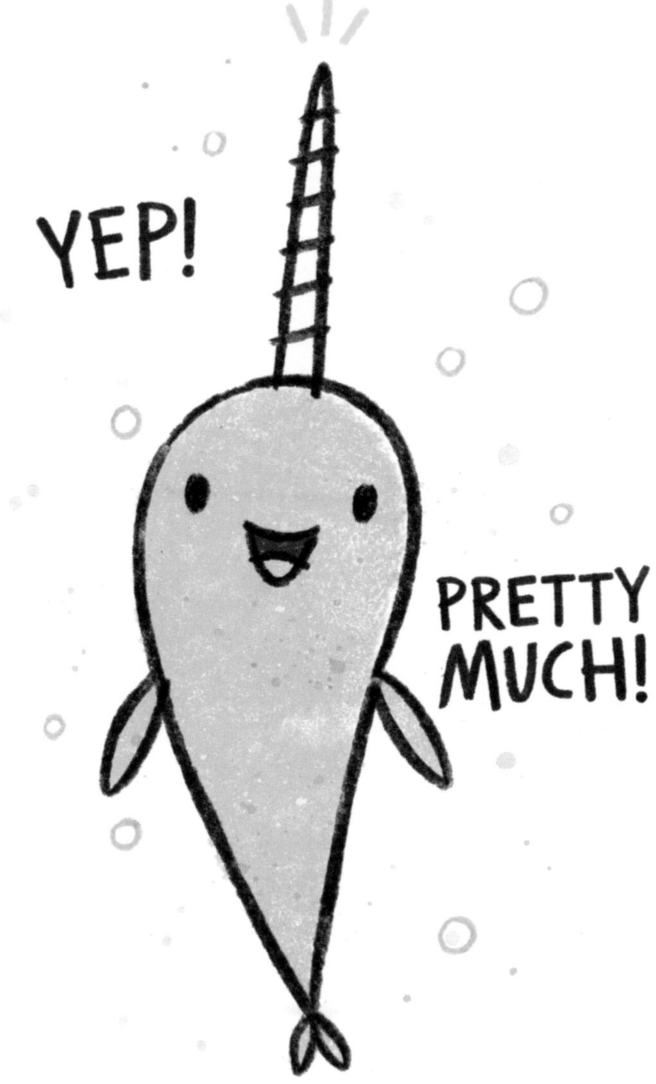
YEP!
PRETTY MUCH!

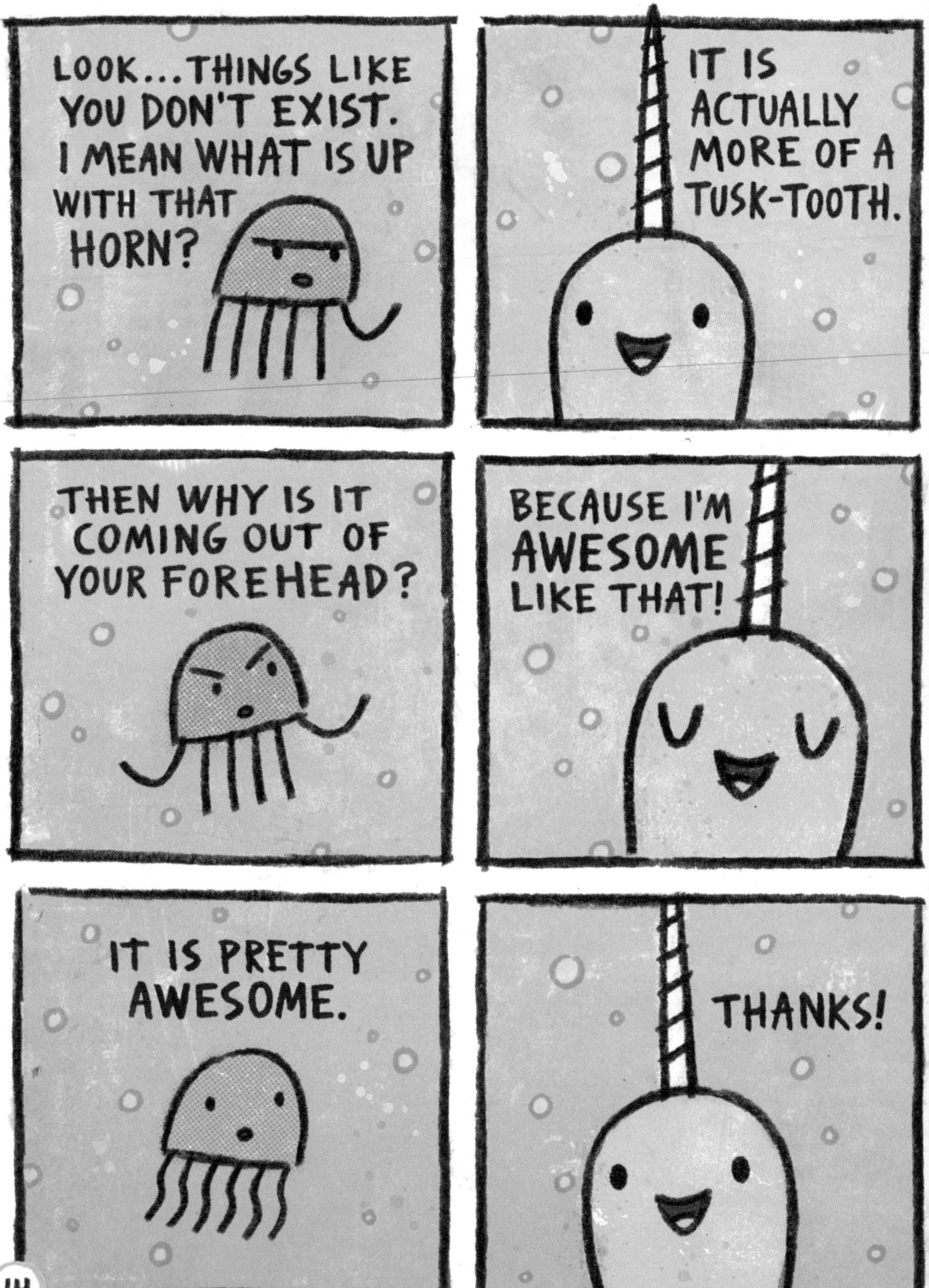
LOOK... THINGS LIKE YOU DON'T EXIST. I MEAN WHAT IS UP WITH THAT HORN?
IT IS ACTUALLY MORE OF A TUSK-TOOTH.
THEN WHY IS IT COMING OUT OF YOUR FOREHEAD?
BECAUSE I'M AWESOME LIKE THAT!
IT IS PRETTY AWESOME.
THANKS!

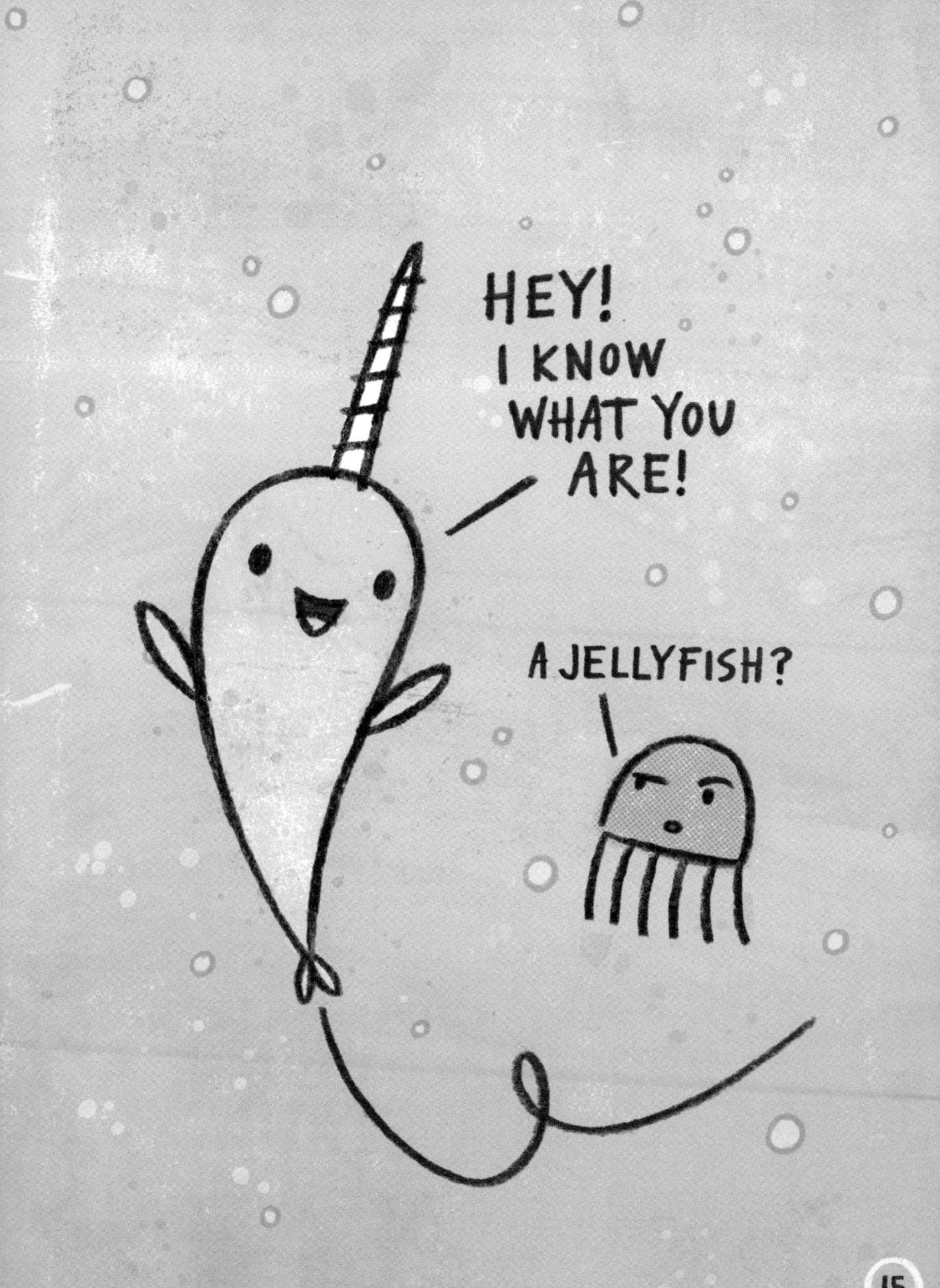
HEY! I KNOW WHAT YOU ARE!
A JELLYFISH?

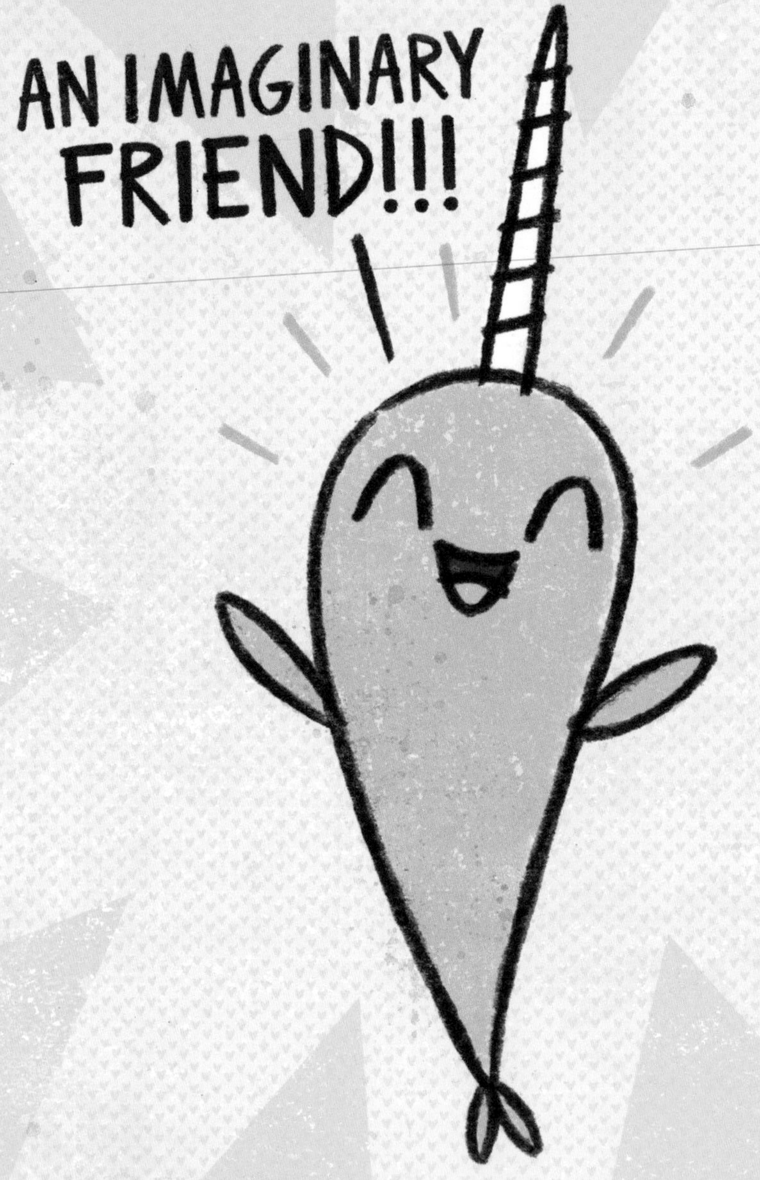
AN IMAGINARY FRIEND!!!

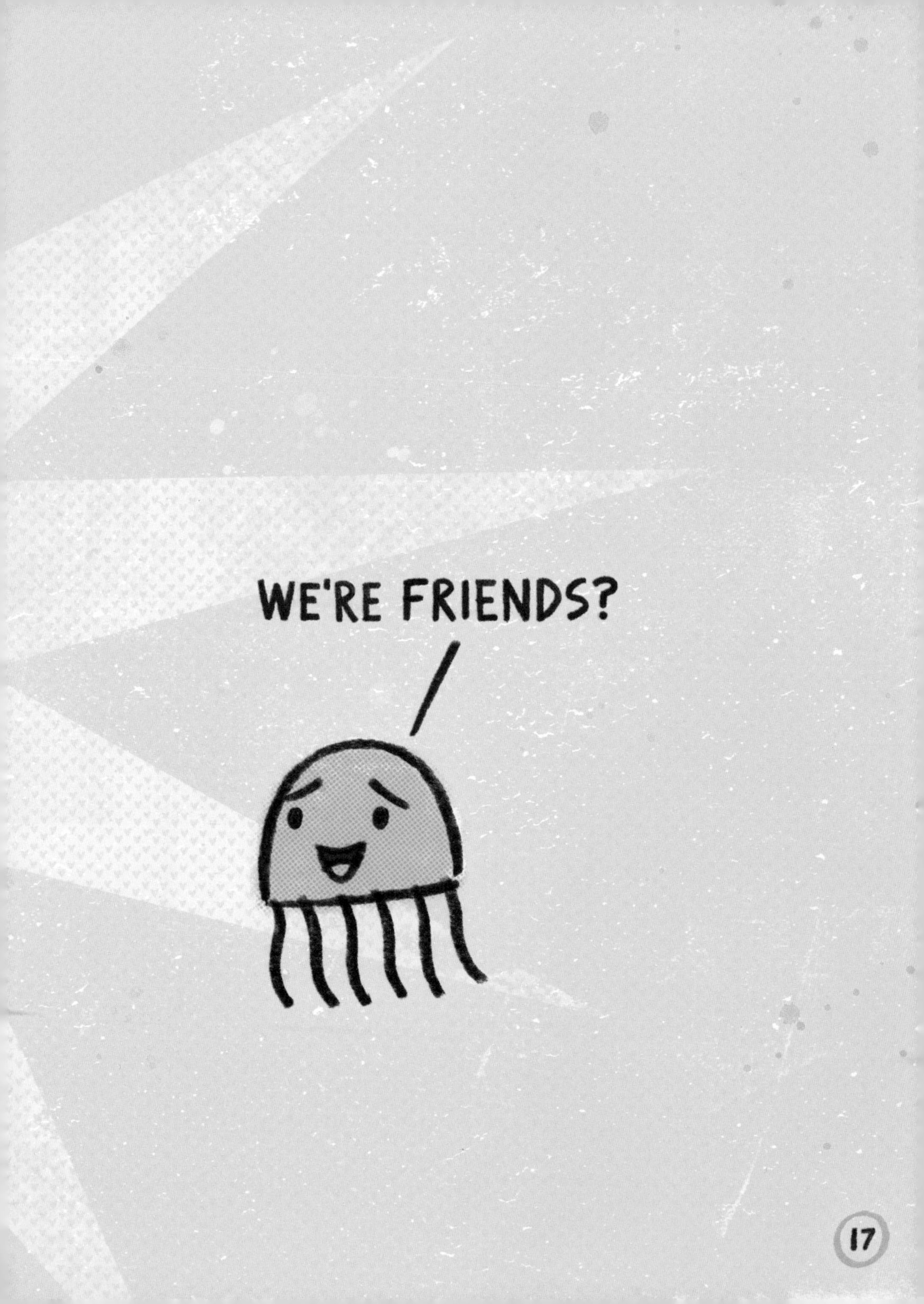
WE'RE FRIENDS?

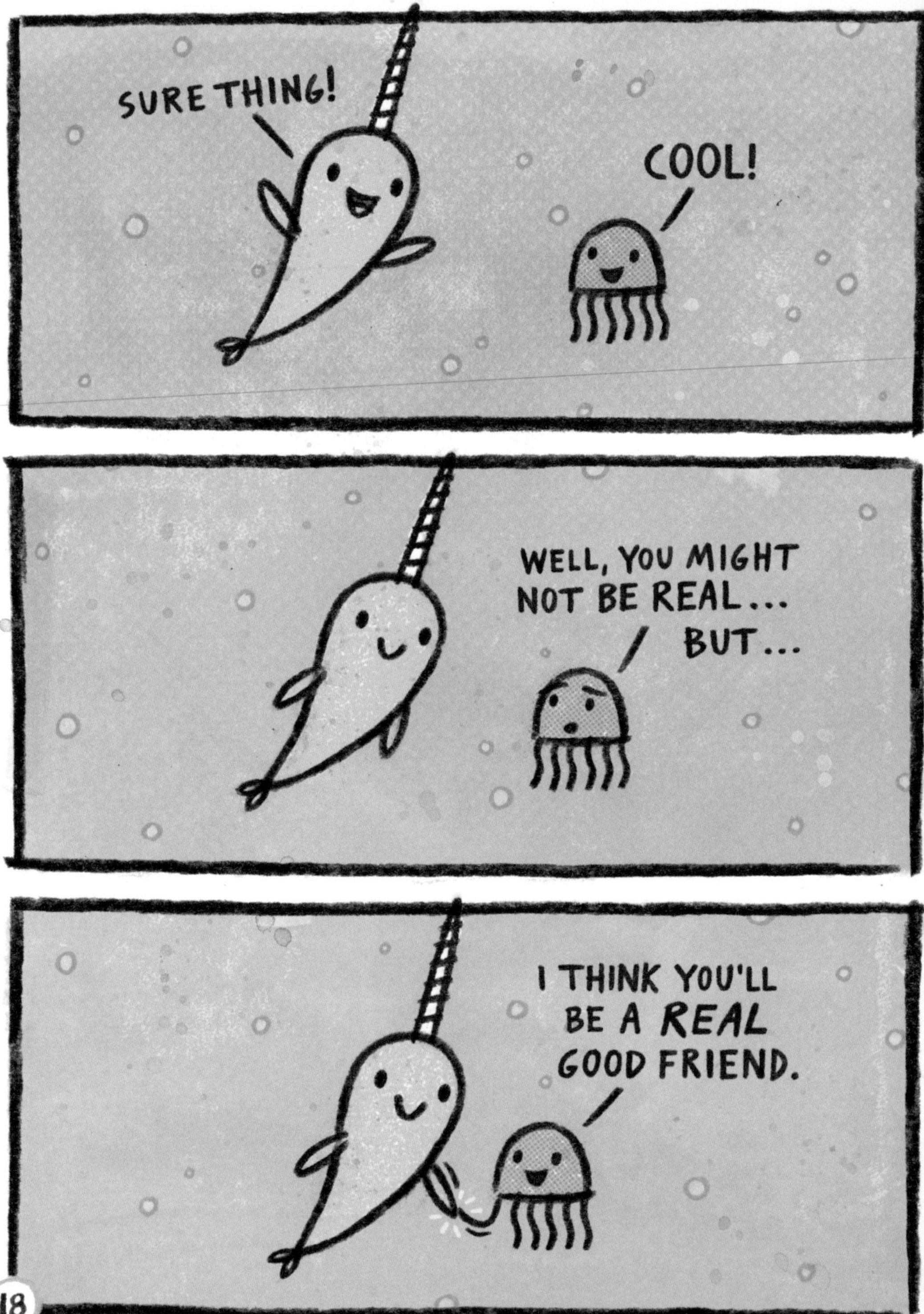
SURE THING!
COOL!
WELL, YOU MIGHT NOT BE REAL... BUT...
I THINK YOU'LL BE A *REAL* GOOD FRIEND.

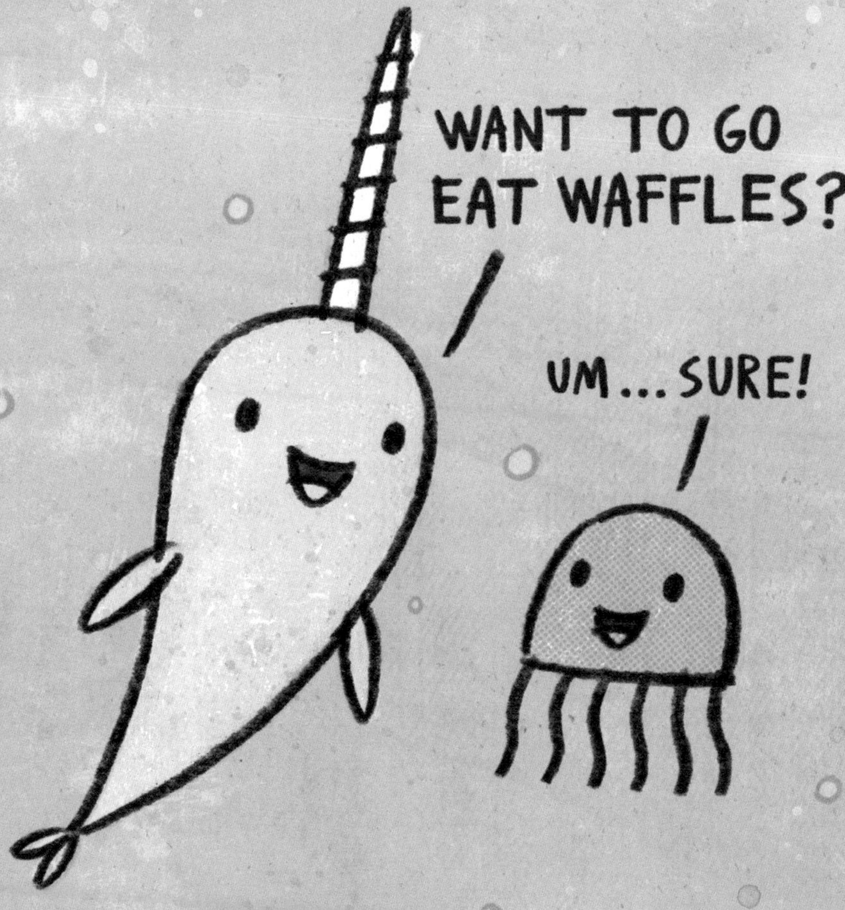
WANT TO GO EAT WAFFLES?
UM... SURE!

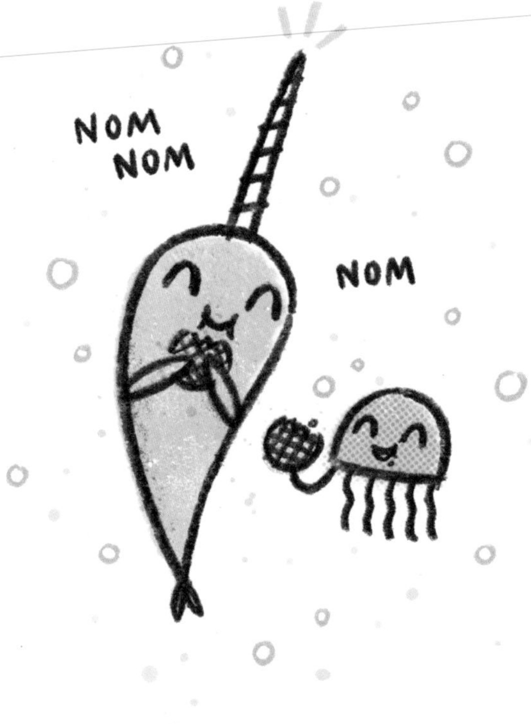
NOM
NOM
NOM

# REALly FUN FACTS

A NARWHAL'S LONG, HORN-LIKE TOOTH CAN REACH UP TO 3 m (10 ft.) LONG!

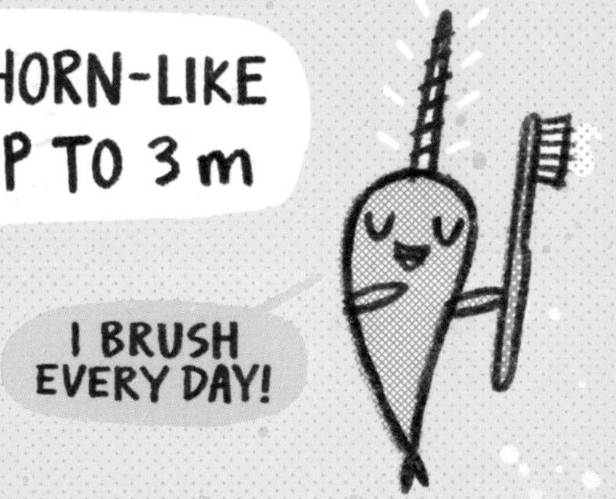
I BRUSH EVERY DAY!

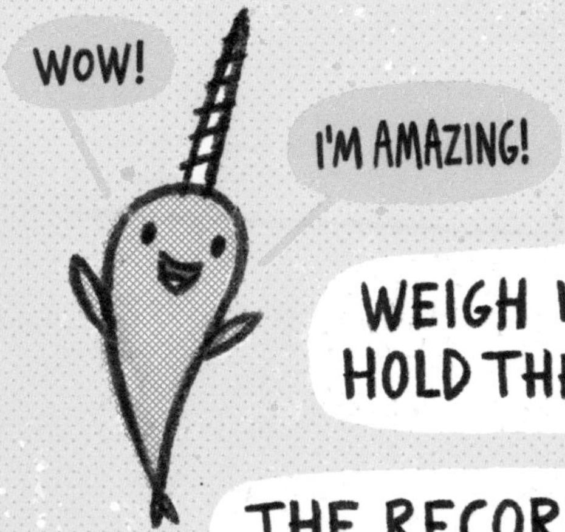
WOW!
I'M AMAZING!

NARWHALS CAN WEIGH 1,600 kg (3,500 lb.) AND HOLD THEIR BREATH FOR 25 min.

THE RECORD DIVE DEPTH FOR A NARWHAL IS 1,800 m (5,905 ft., OVER ONE MILE).

RECENT RESEARCH SUGGESTS NARWHALS CAN LIVE UP TO 90 YEARS.

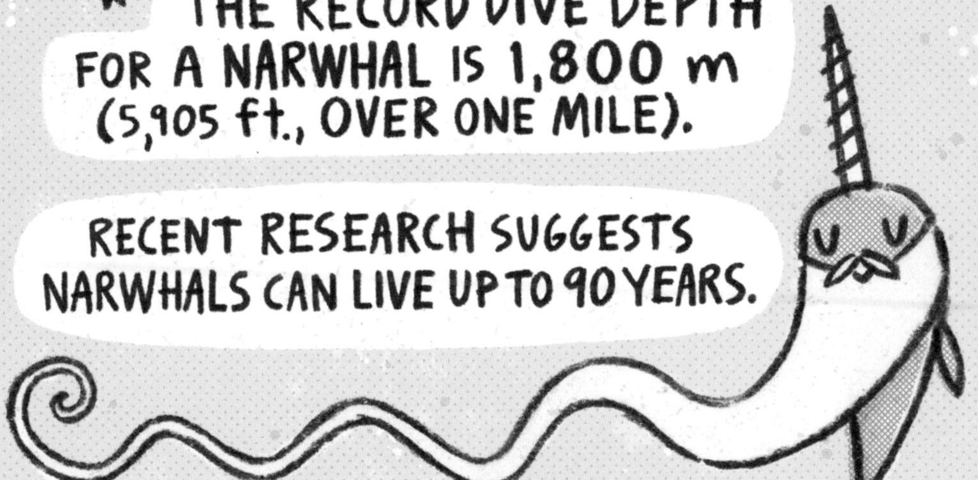

# MORE REALly FUN FACTS

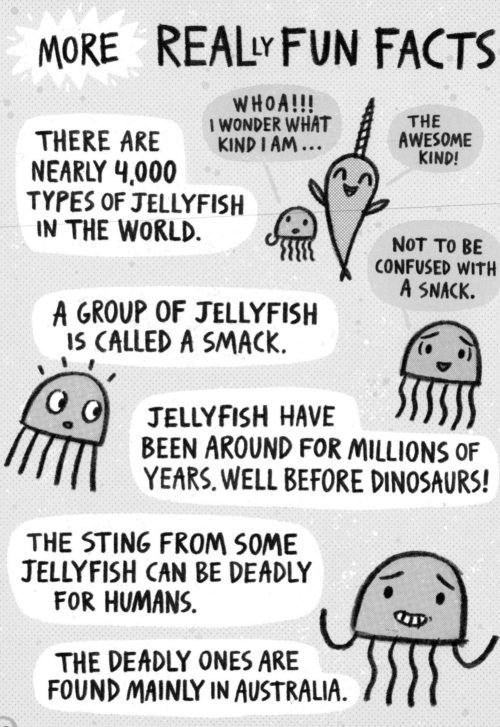

WHOA!!! I WONDER WHAT KIND I AM...

THE AWESOME KIND!

THERE ARE NEARLY 4,000 TYPES OF JELLYFISH IN THE WORLD.

NOT TO BE CONFUSED WITH A SNACK.

A GROUP OF JELLYFISH IS CALLED A SMACK.

JELLYFISH HAVE BEEN AROUND FOR MILLIONS OF YEARS. WELL BEFORE DINOSAURS!

THE STING FROM SOME JELLYFISH CAN BE DEADLY FOR HUMANS.

THE DEADLY ONES ARE FOUND MAINLY IN AUSTRALIA.

# NARWHAL'S POD OF AWESOMENESS

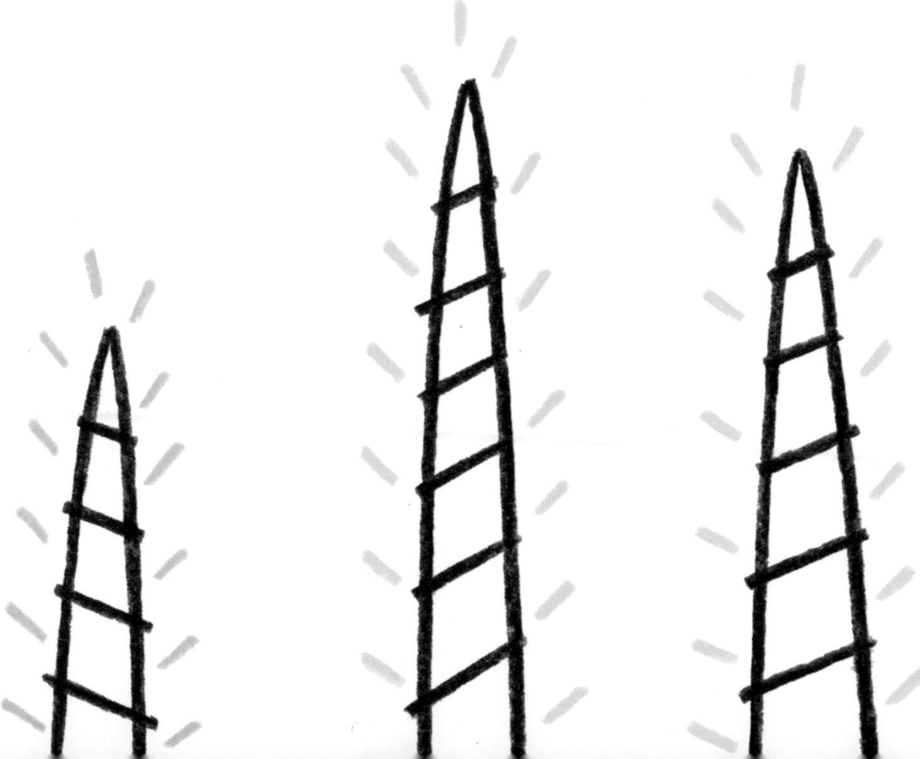

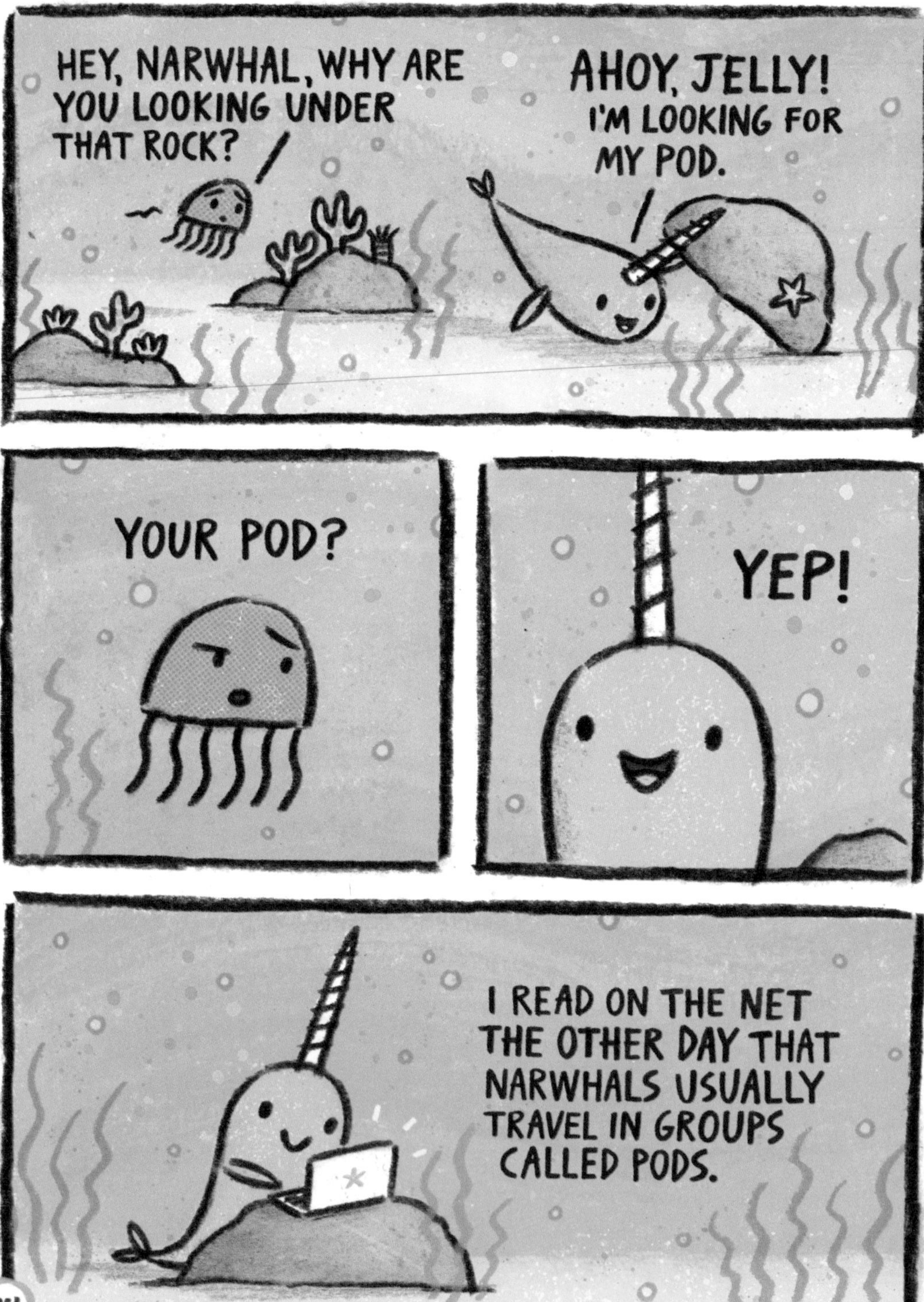
HEY, NARWHAL, WHY ARE YOU LOOKING UNDER THAT ROCK?
AHOY, JELLY! I'M LOOKING FOR MY POD.
YOUR POD?
YEP!
I READ ON THE NET THE OTHER DAY THAT NARWHALS USUALLY TRAVEL IN GROUPS CALLED PODS.

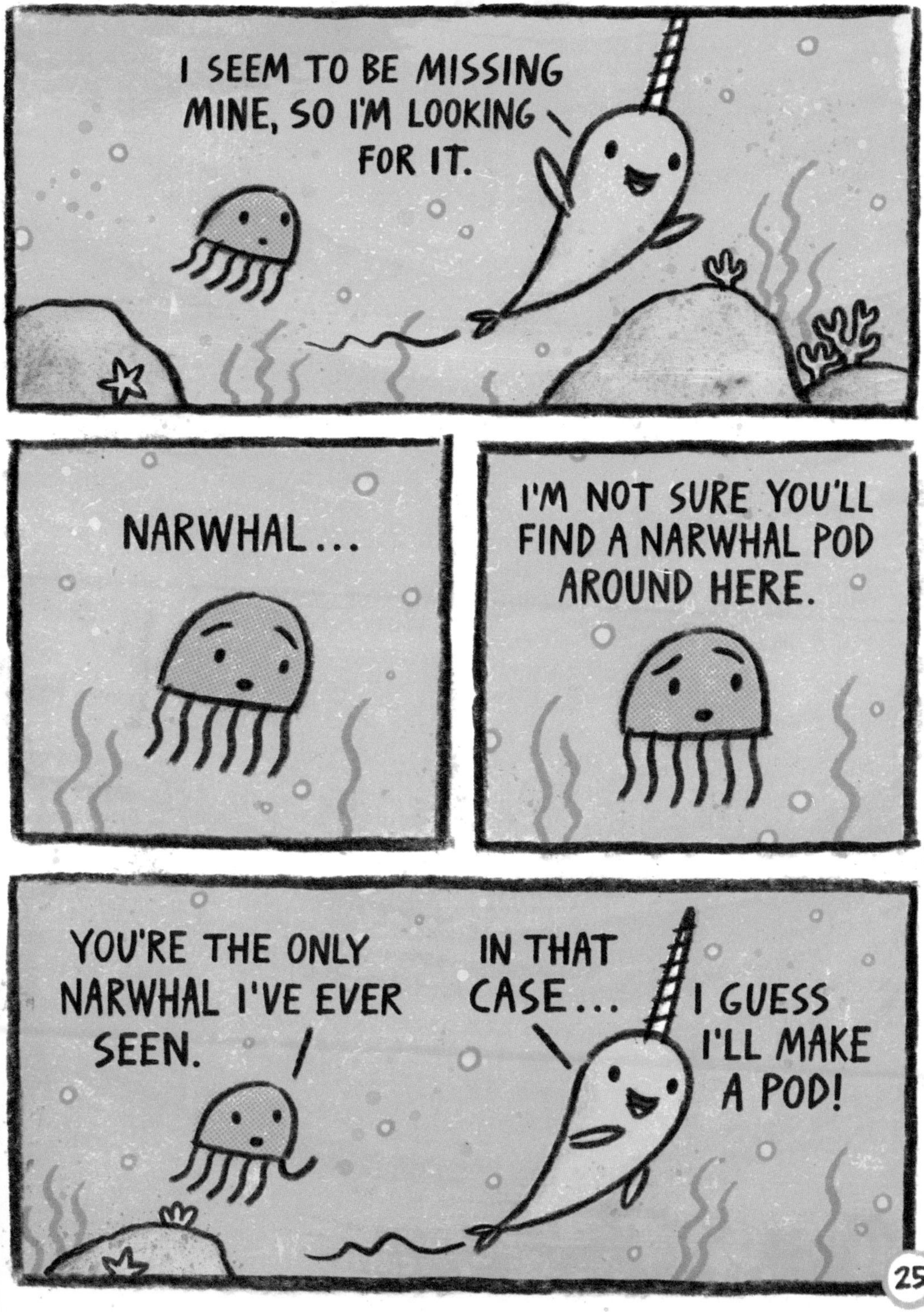
I SEEM TO BE MISSING MINE, SO I'M LOOKING FOR IT.
NARWHAL...
I'M NOT SURE YOU'LL FIND A NARWHAL POD AROUND HERE.
YOU'RE THE ONLY NARWHAL I'VE EVER SEEN.
IN THAT CASE...
I GUESS I'LL MAKE A POD!

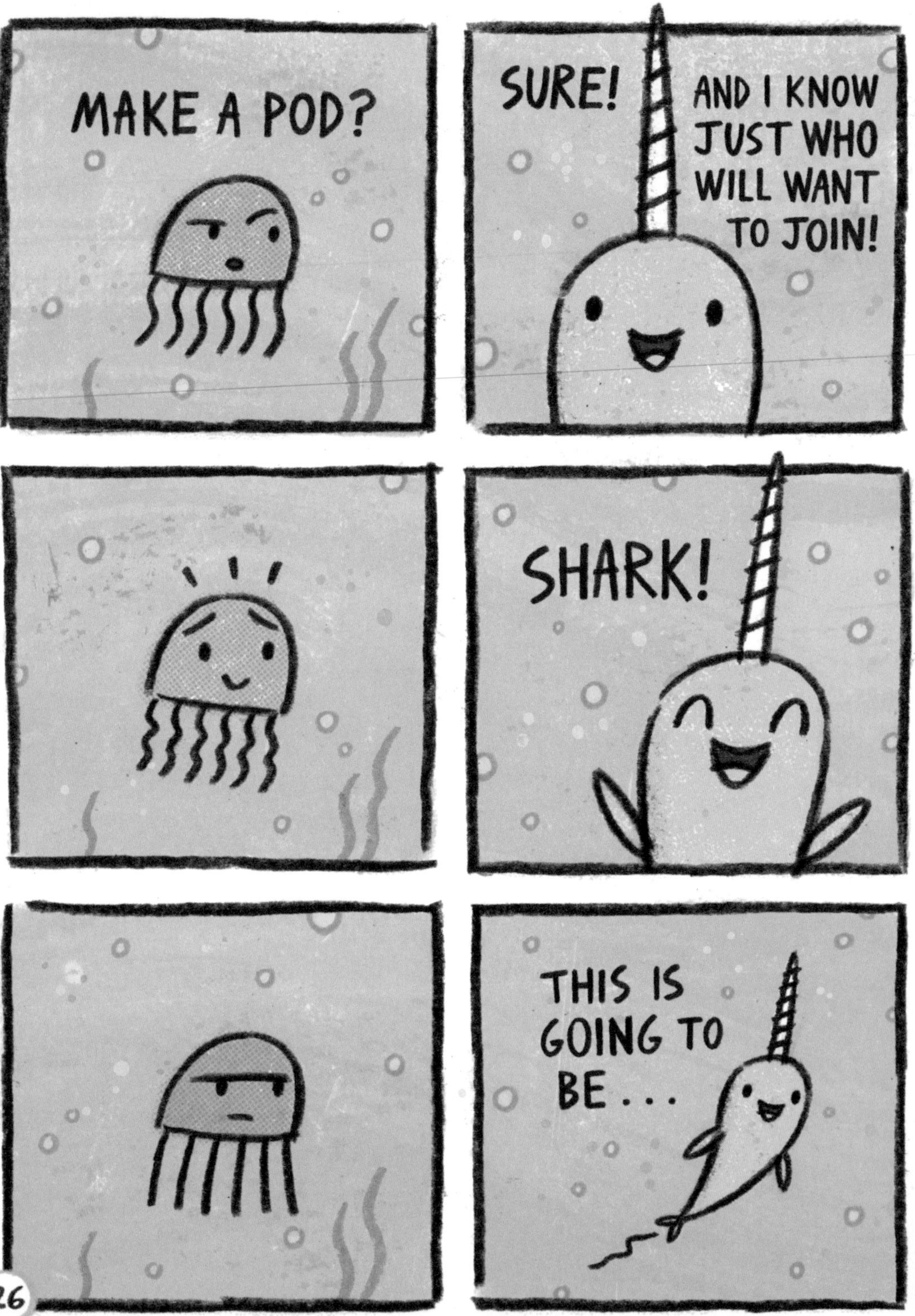
MAKE A POD?
SURE!
AND I KNOW JUST WHO WILL WANT TO JOIN!
SHARK!
THIS IS GOING TO BE...

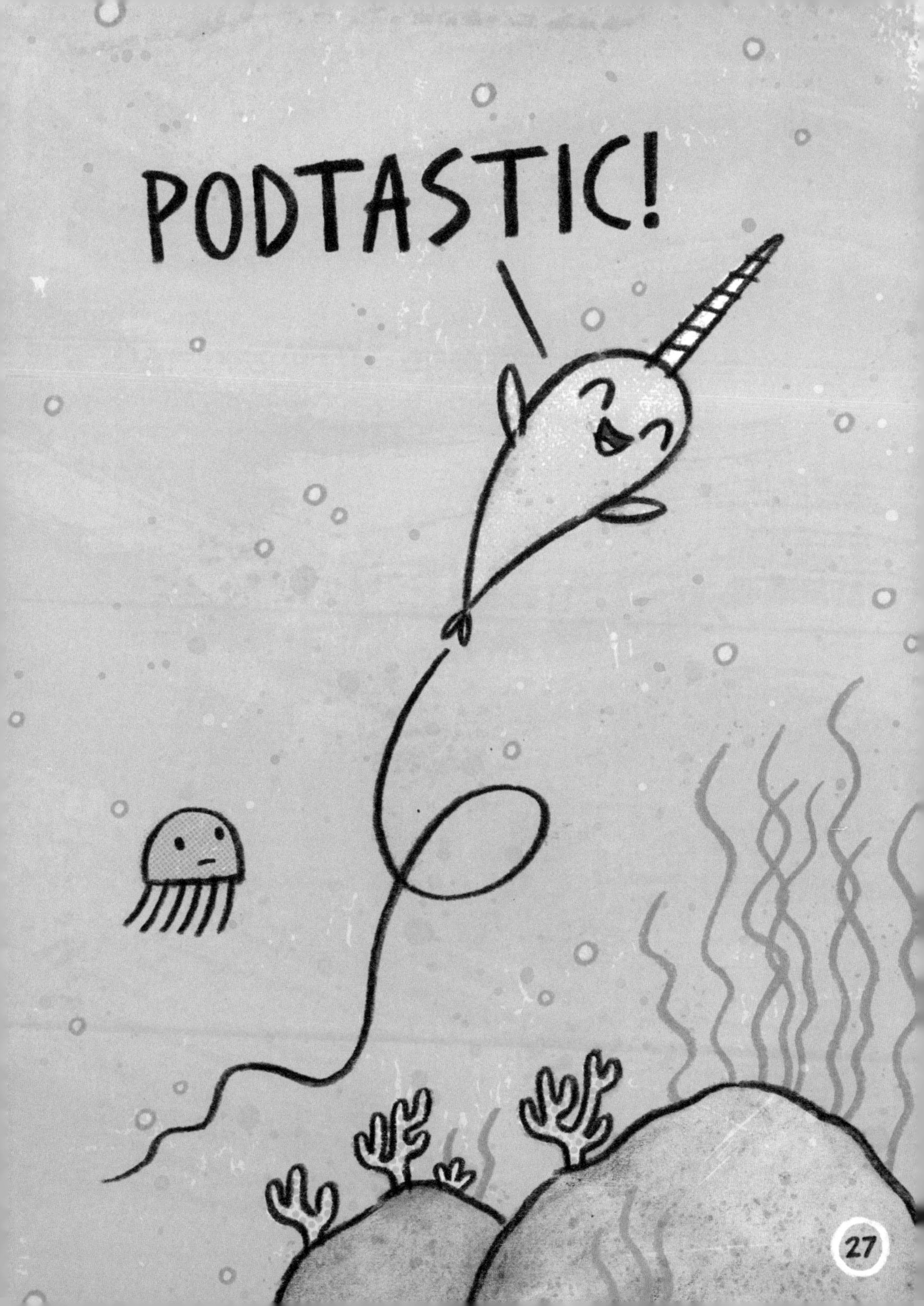
PODTASTIC!

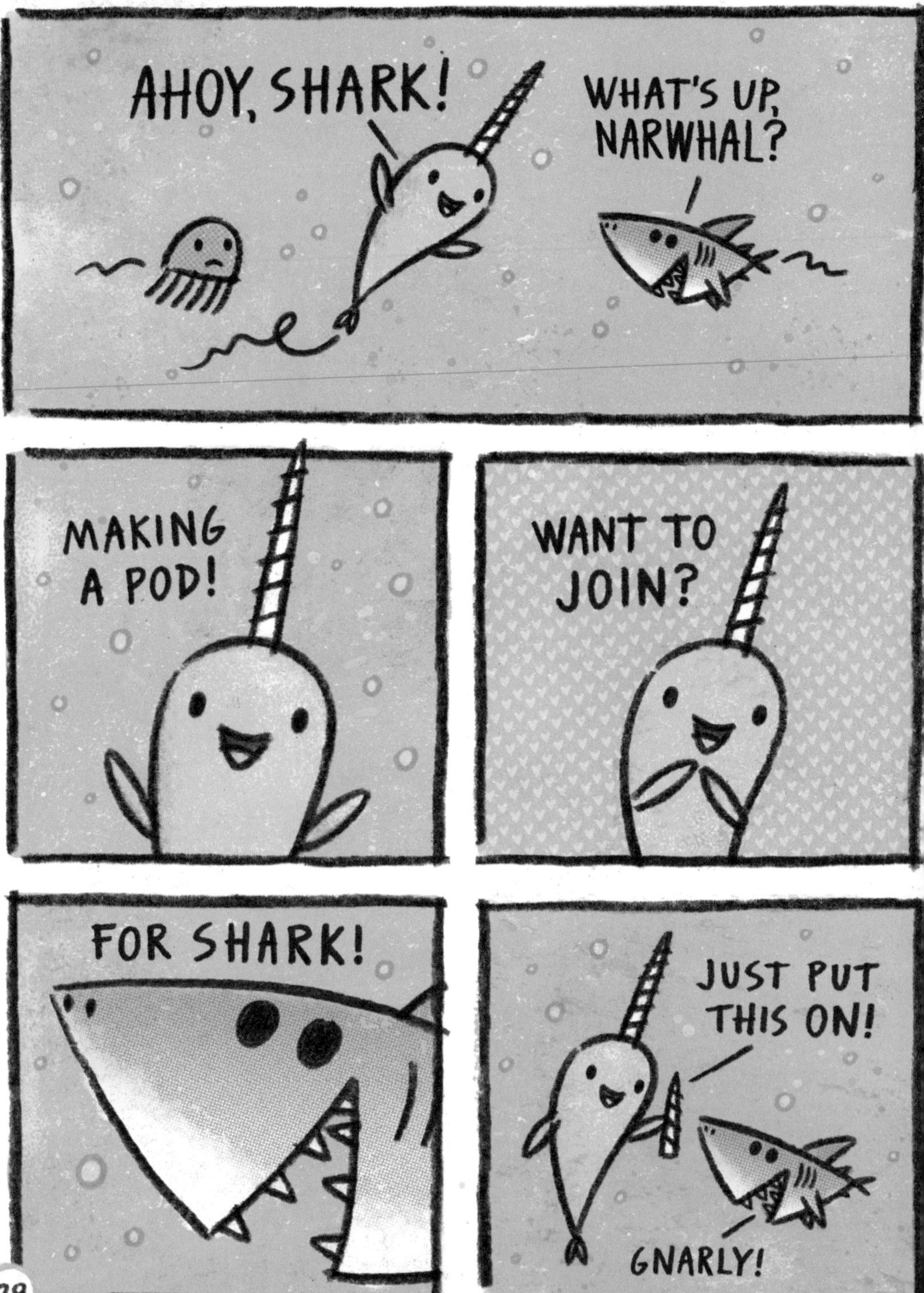

AHOY, SHARK!
WHAT'S UP, NARWHAL?
MAKING A POD!
WANT TO JOIN?
FOR SHARK!
JUST PUT THIS ON!
GNARLY!

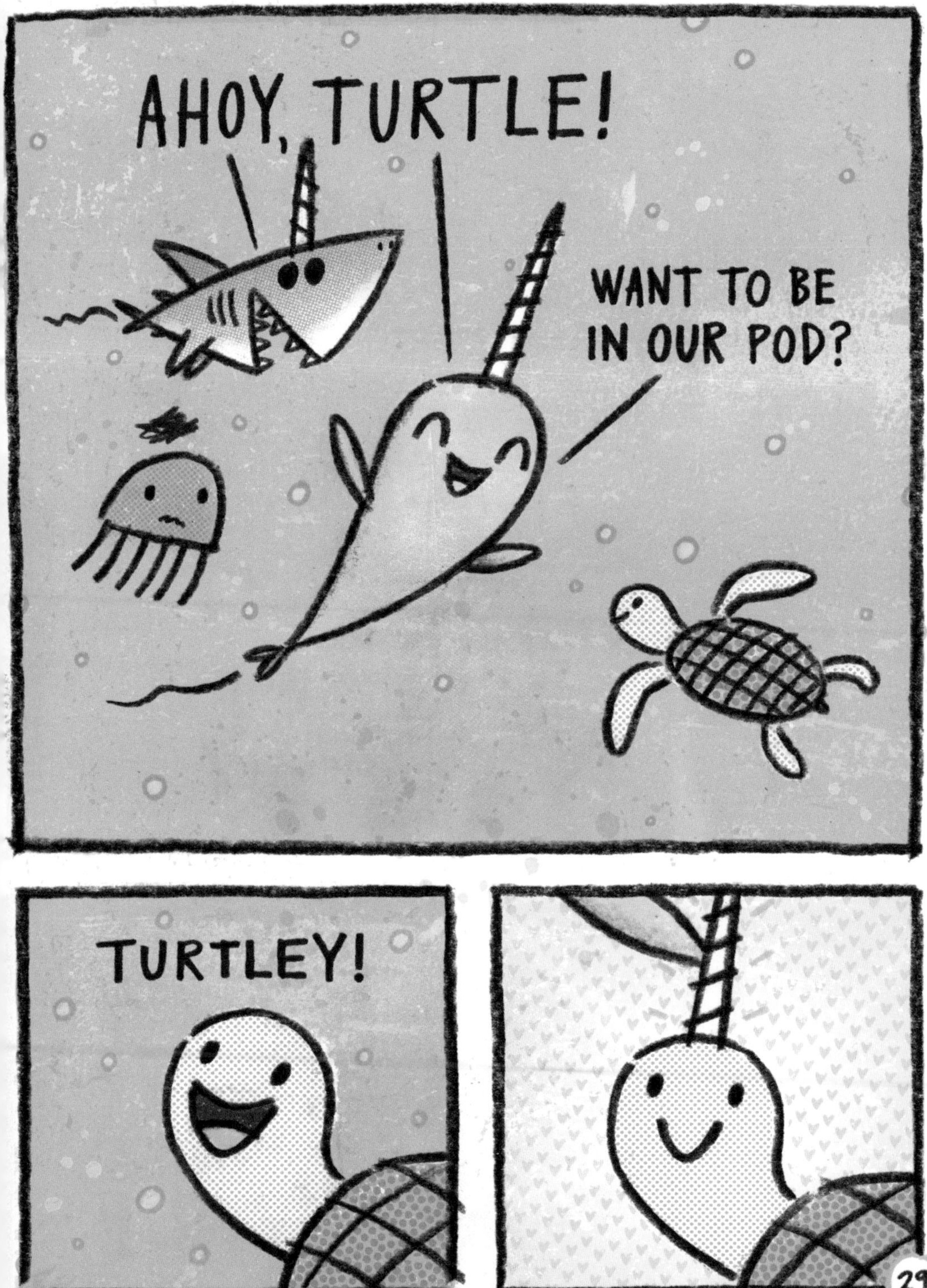
AHOY, TURTLE!
WANT TO BE IN OUR POD?
TURTLEY!

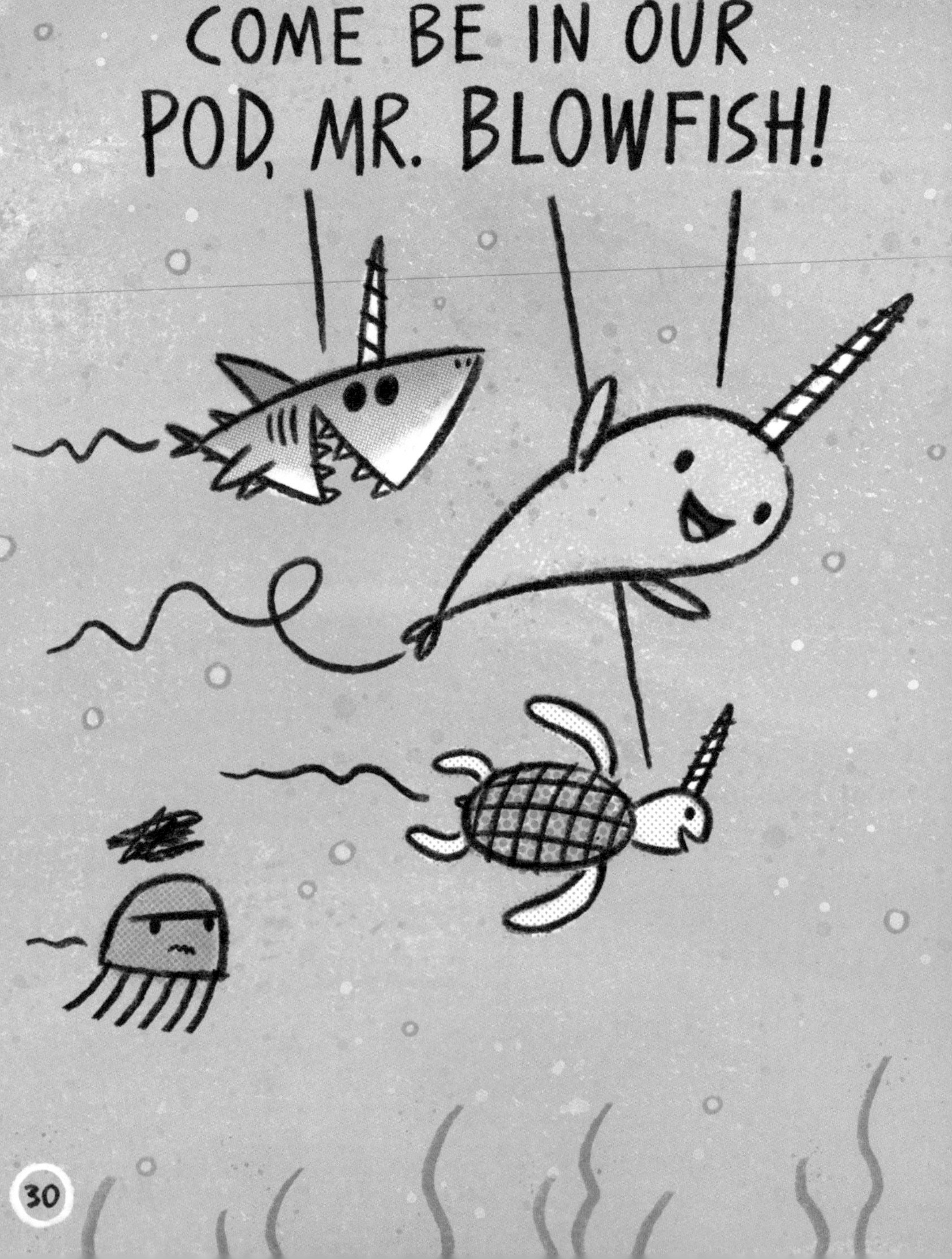
COME BE IN OUR POD, MR. BLOWFISH!

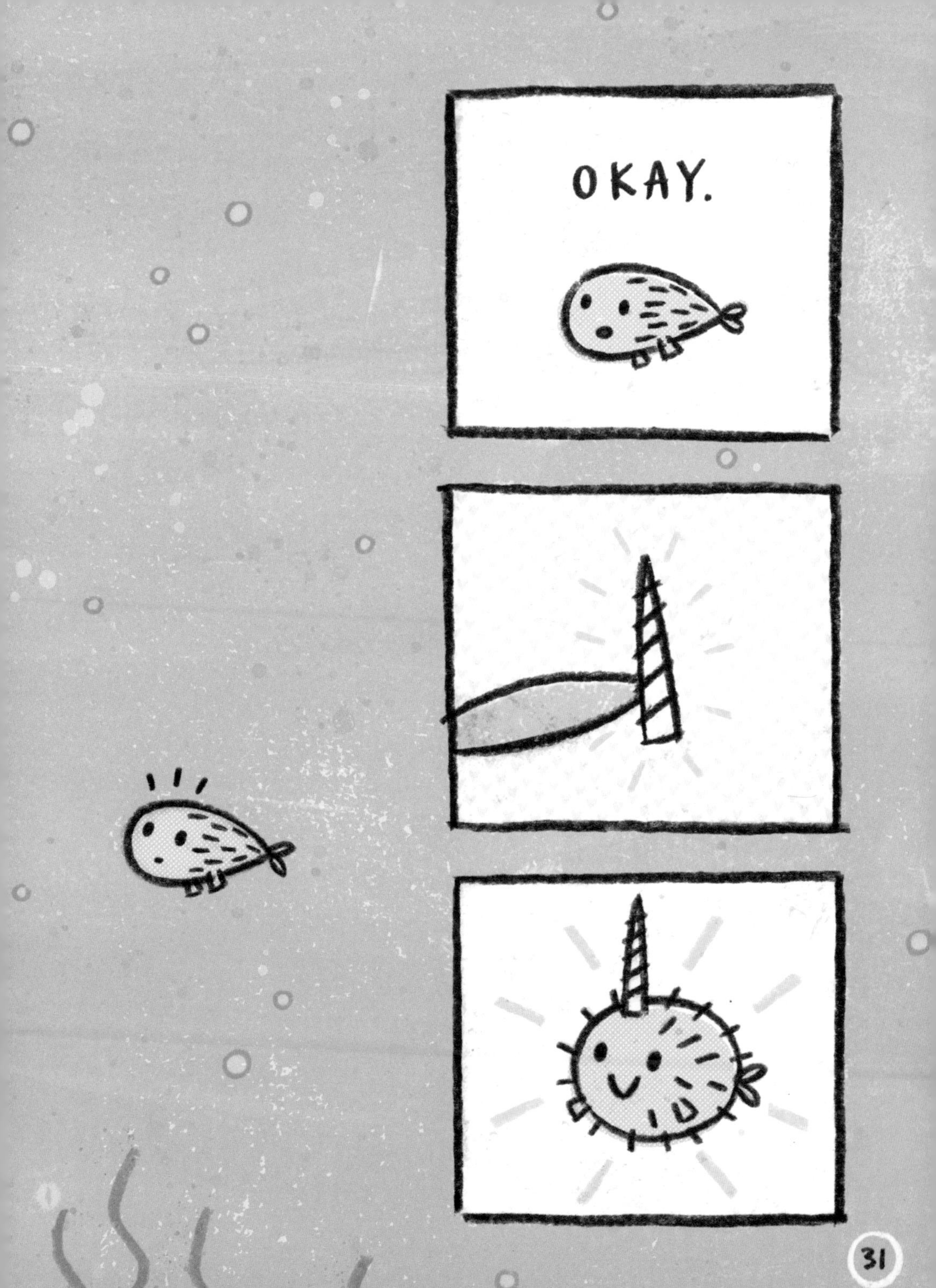
OKAY.

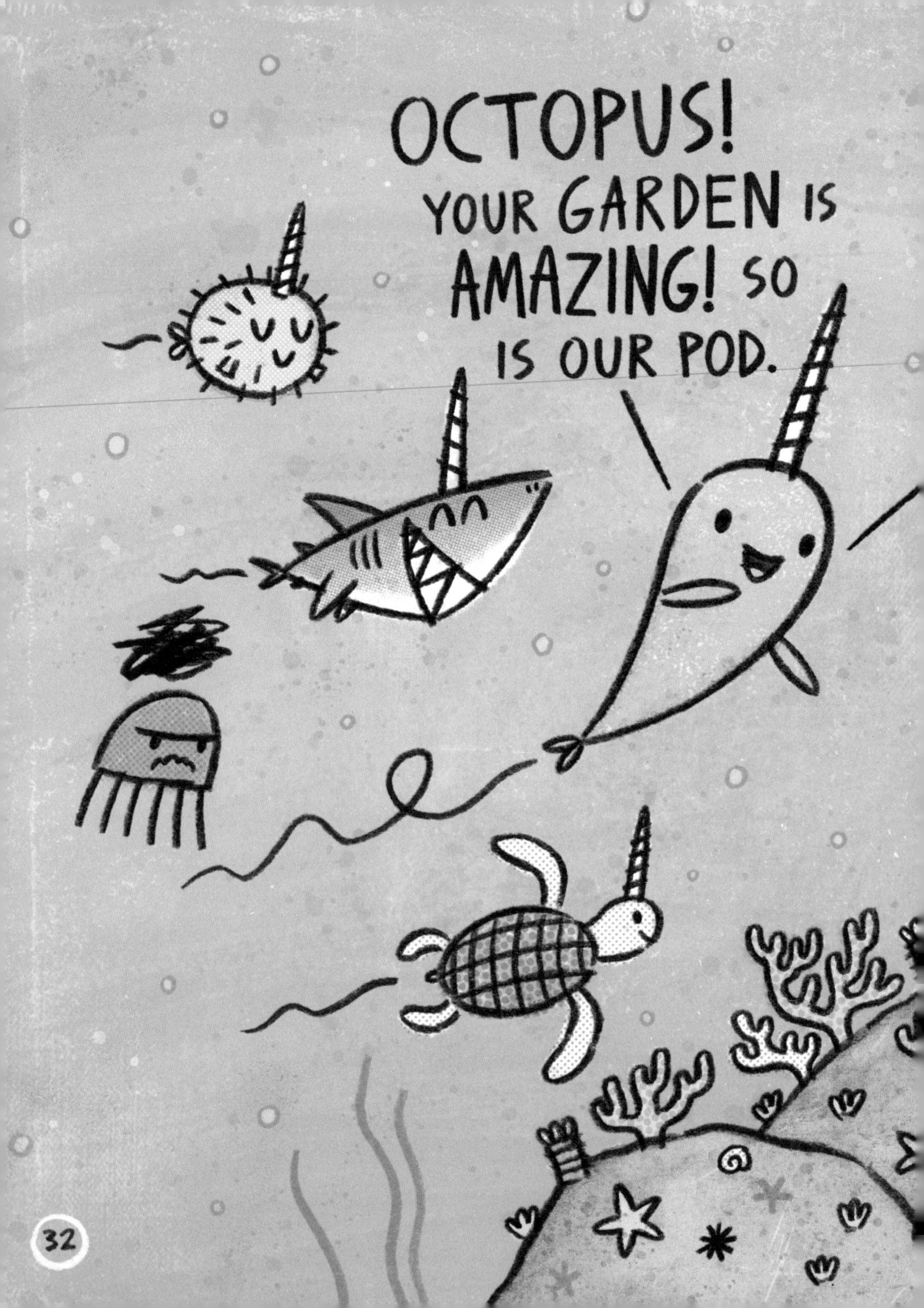
OCTOPUS! YOUR GARDEN IS AMAZING! SO IS OUR POD.

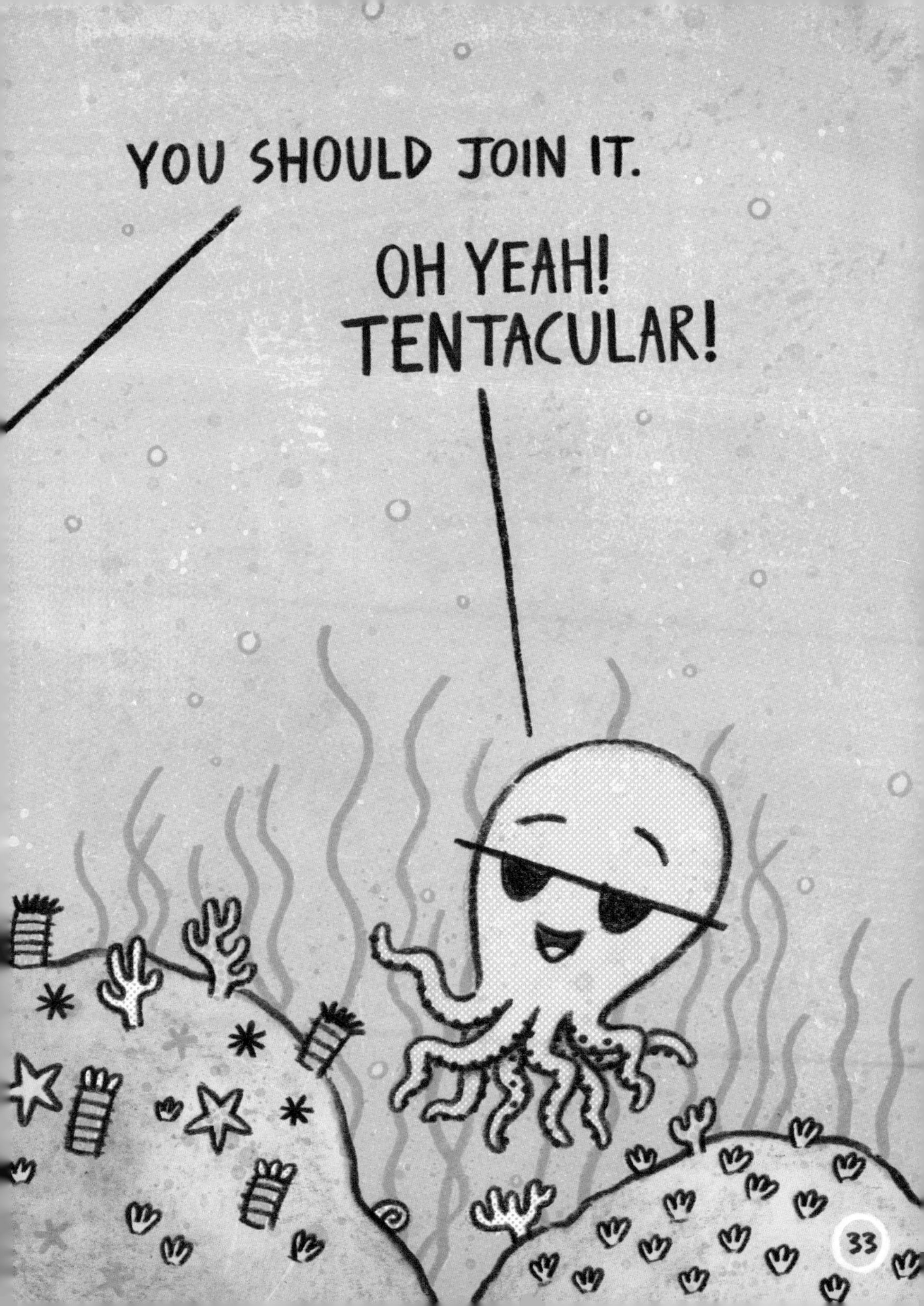
YOU SHOULD JOIN IT.
OH YEAH! TENTACULAR!

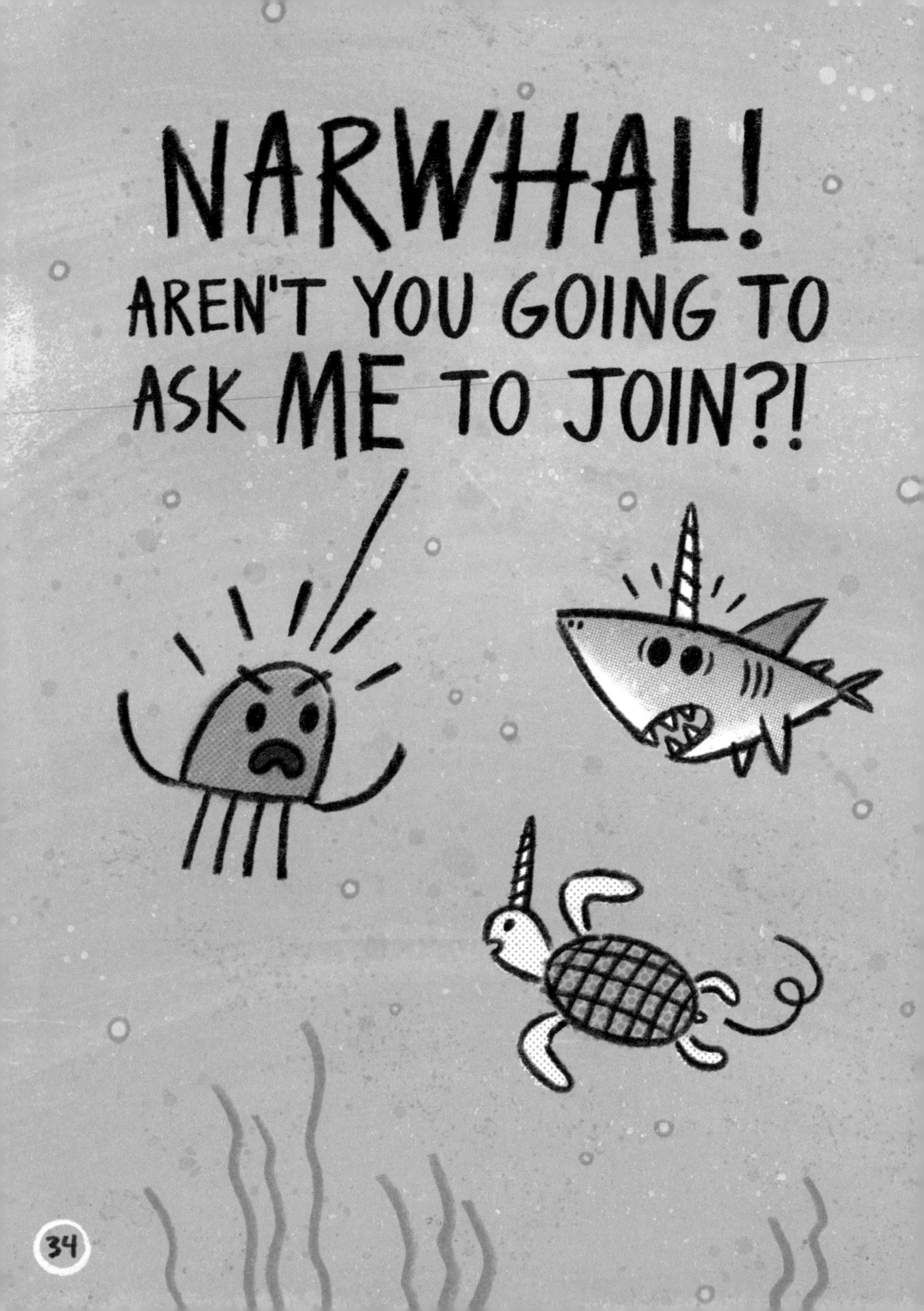
NARWHAL!
AREN'T YOU GOING TO ASK ME TO JOIN?!

OH! I DIDN'T ASK? I GUESS I THOUGHT WE WERE MAKING THE POD TOGETHER. YOU DO WANT TO BE PART OF OUR POD, RIGHT, JELLY?

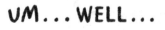

UM... WELL...

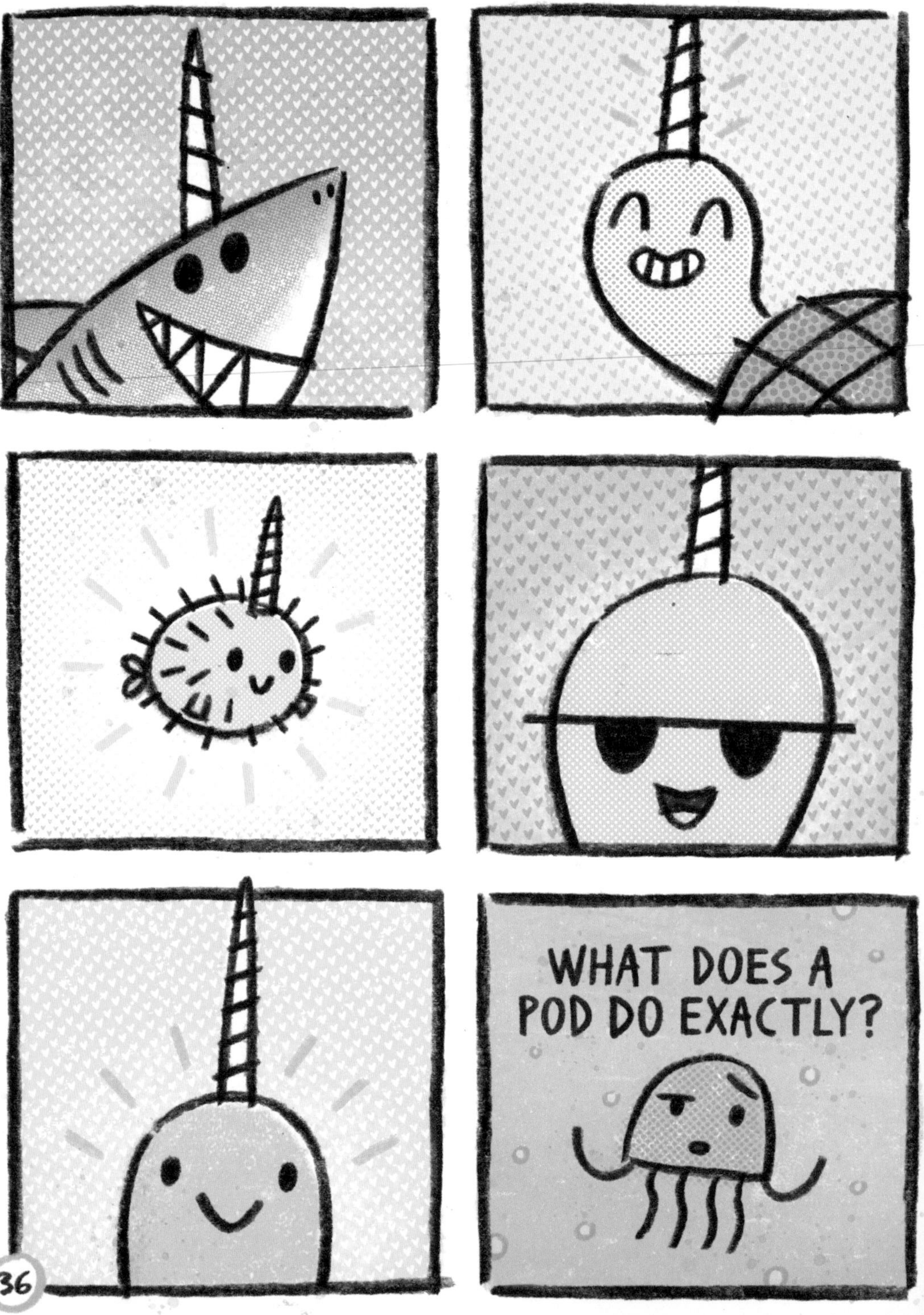
WHAT DOES A POD DO EXACTLY?

# I'M NOT REALLY SURE!

## BUT I IMAGINE A POD PLAYS ULTIMATE CANNONBALL, EATS WAFFLES, FIGHTS CRIME AND...

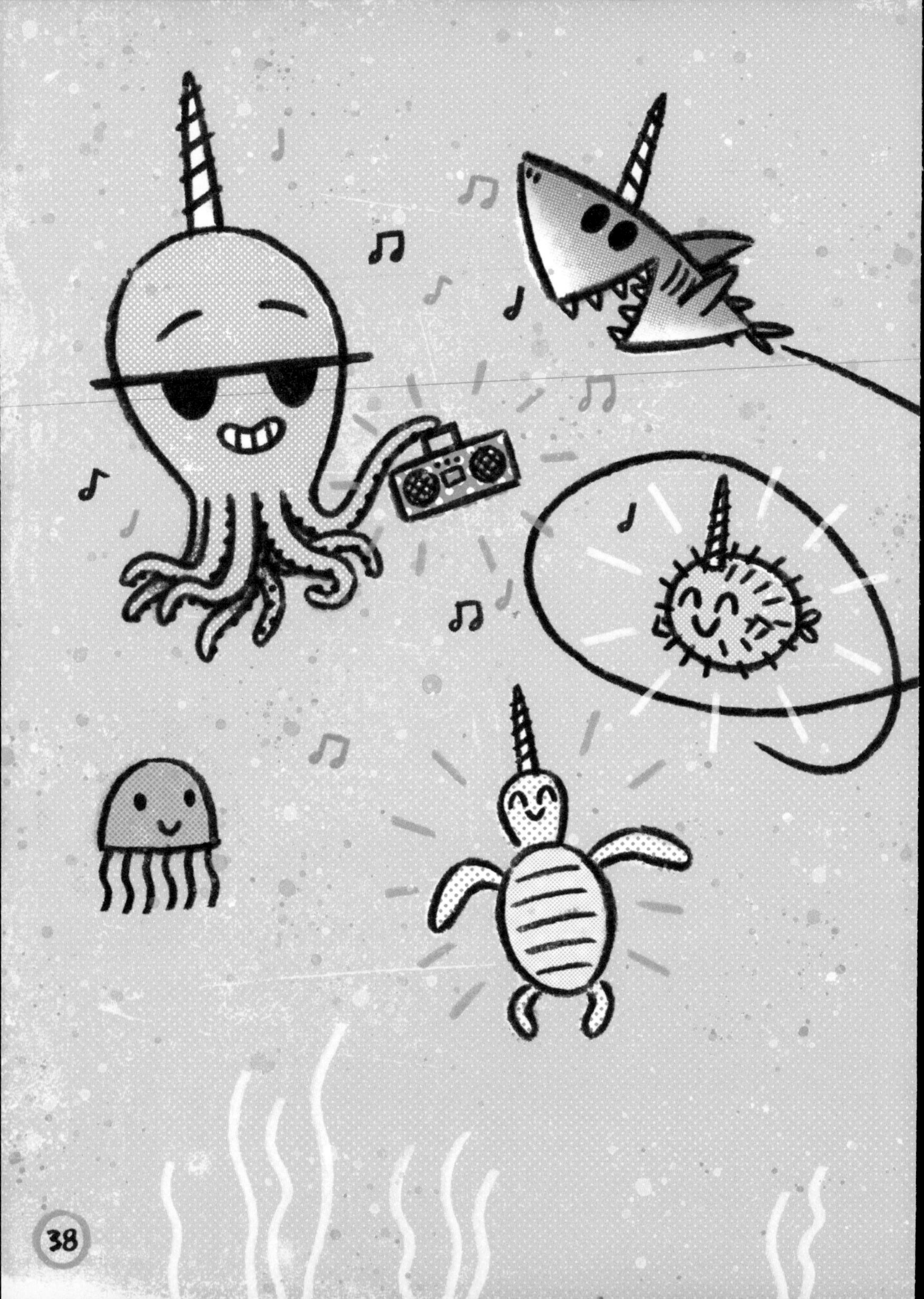

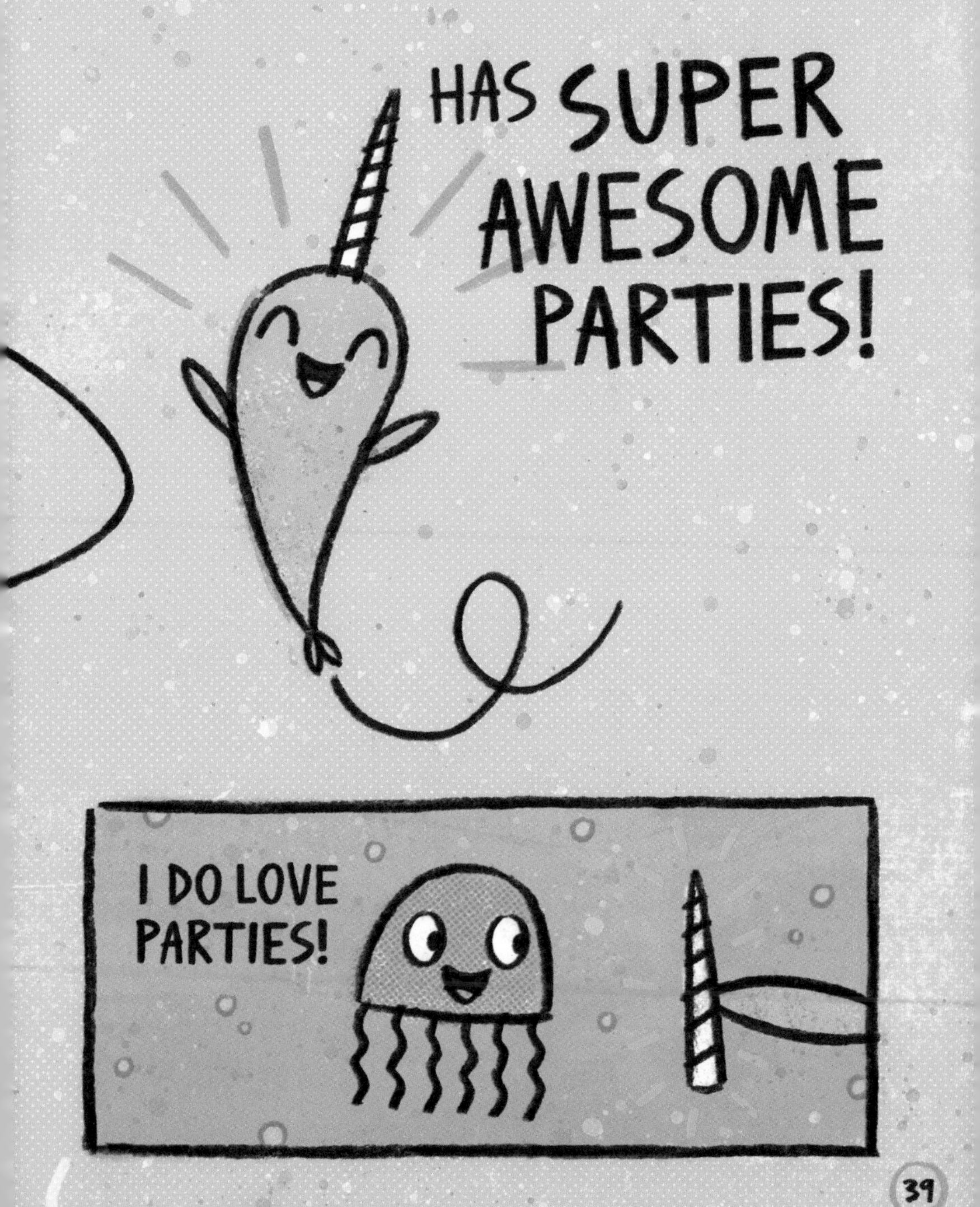
HAS SUPER AWESOME PARTIES!
I DO LOVE PARTIES!

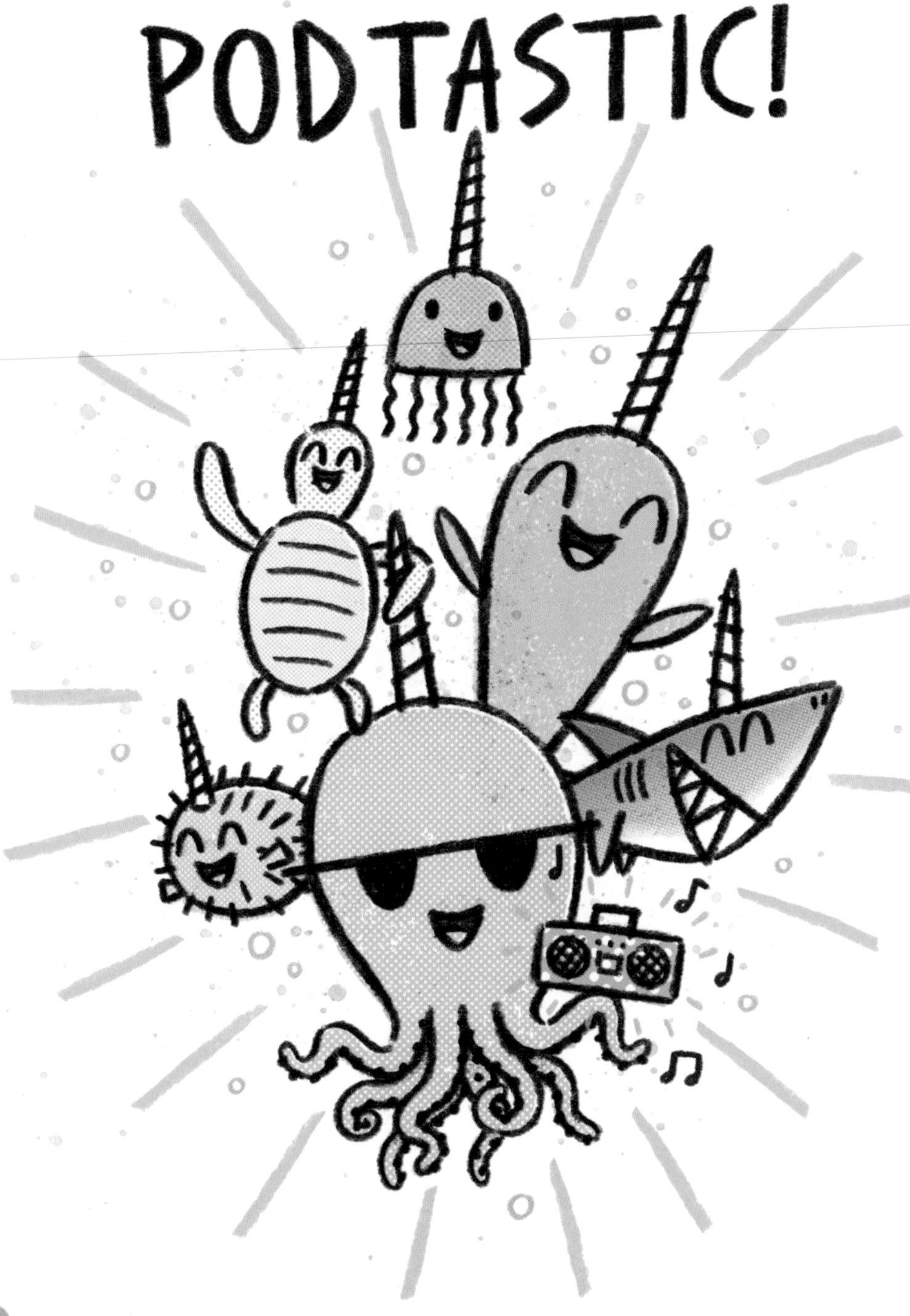
PODTASTIC!

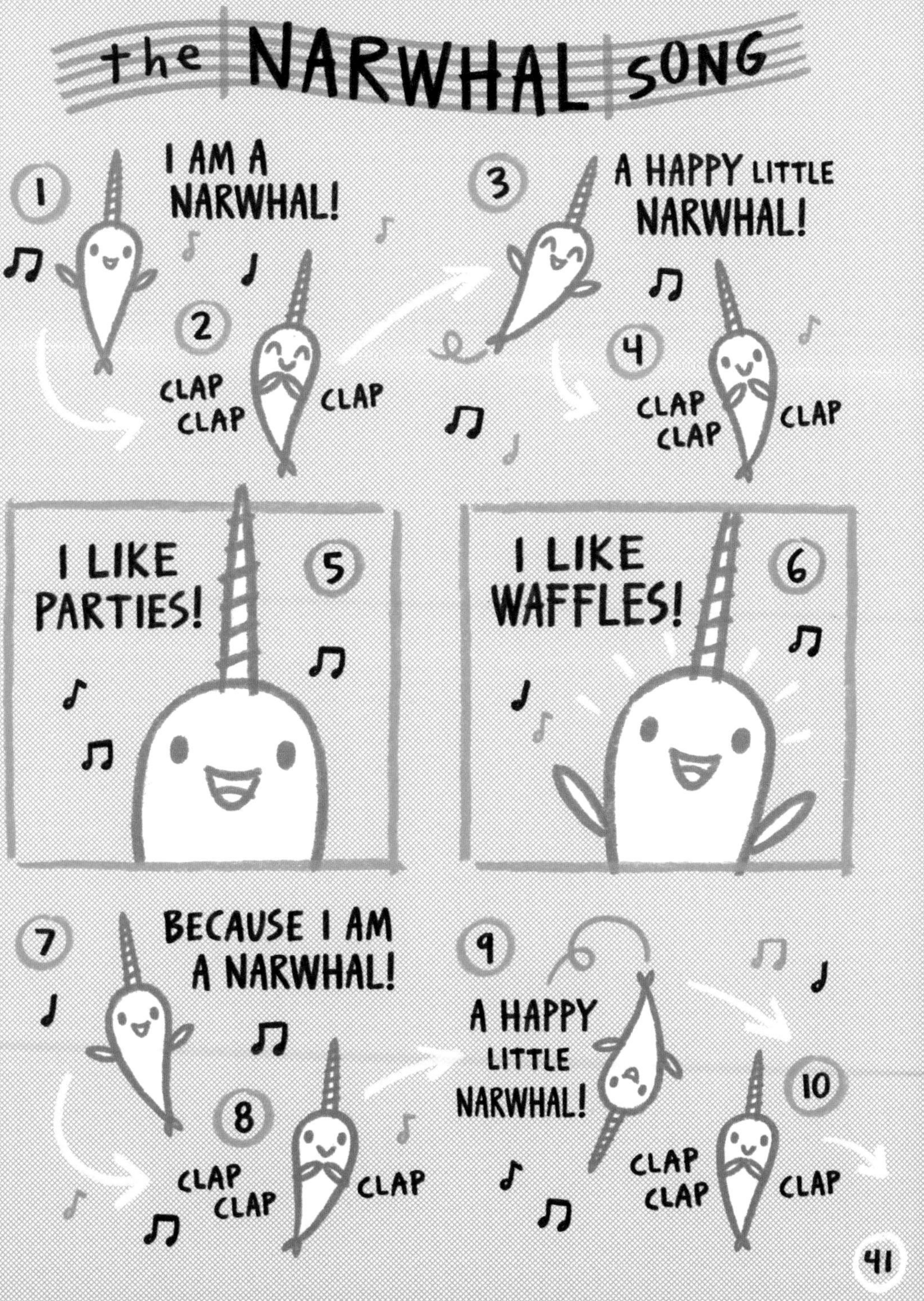
the NARWHAL SONG
1
I AM A NARWHAL!
2
CLAP CLAP
CLAP
3
A HAPPY LITTLE NARWHAL!
4
CLAP CLAP
CLAP
I LIKE PARTIES!
5
I LIKE WAFFLES!
6
7
BECAUSE I AM A NARWHAL!
8
CLAP CLAP
CLAP
9
A HAPPY LITTLE NARWHAL!
10
CLAP CLAP
CLAP

# NARWHAL!

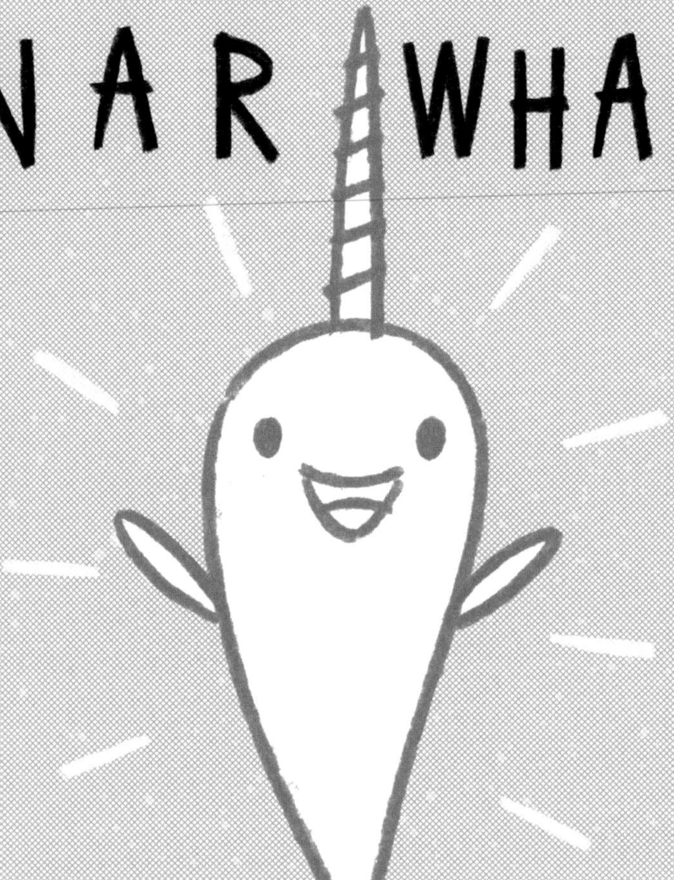

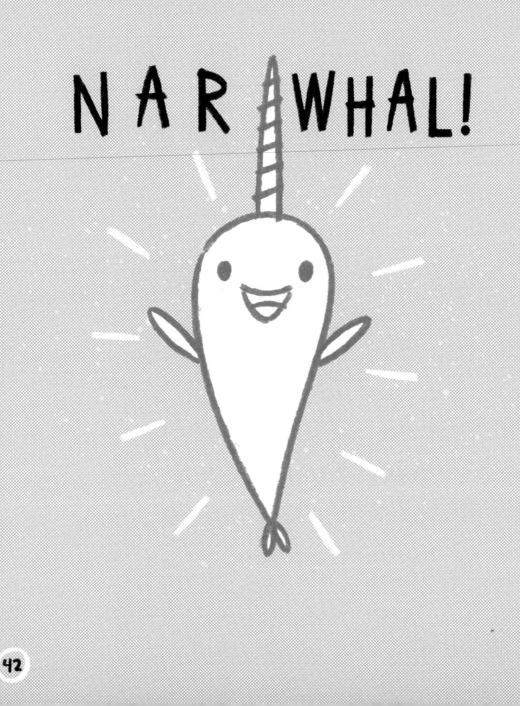

# NARWHAL
## AND THE
# BEST
# BOOK
# EVER!

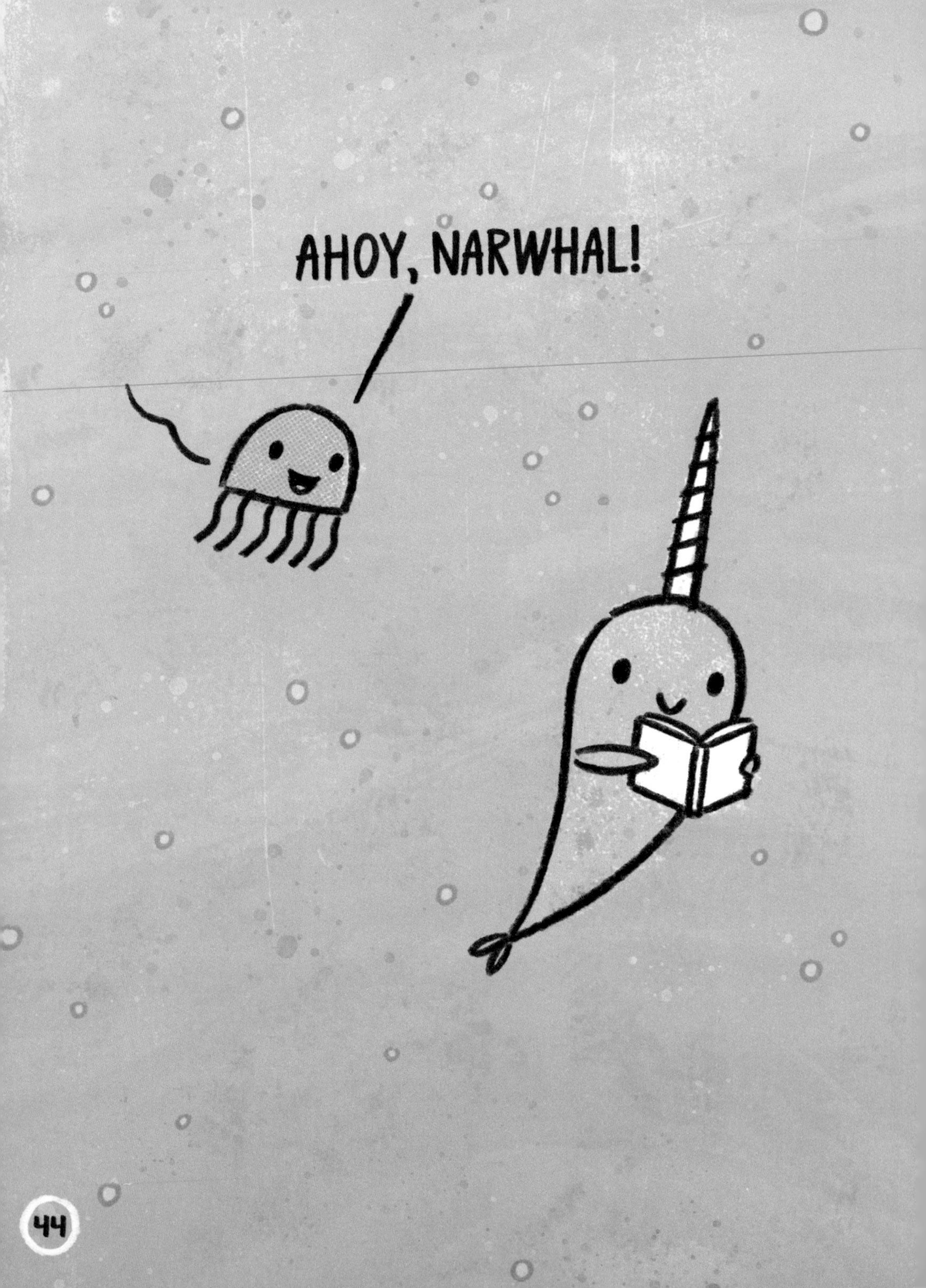
AHOY, NARWHAL!

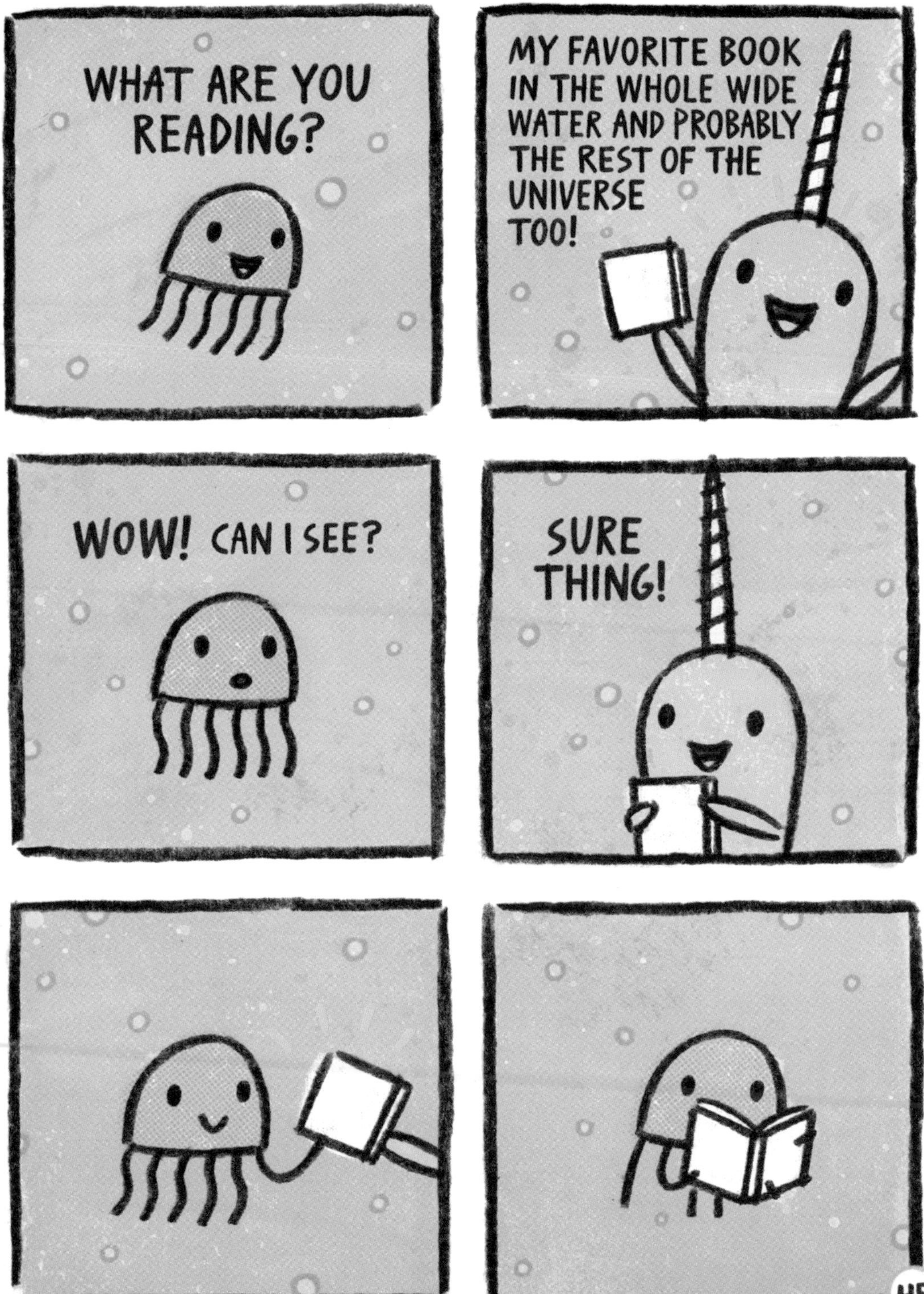
WHAT ARE YOU READING?
MY FAVORITE BOOK IN THE WHOLE WIDE WATER AND PROBABLY THE REST OF THE UNIVERSE TOO!
WOW! CAN I SEE?
SURE THING!

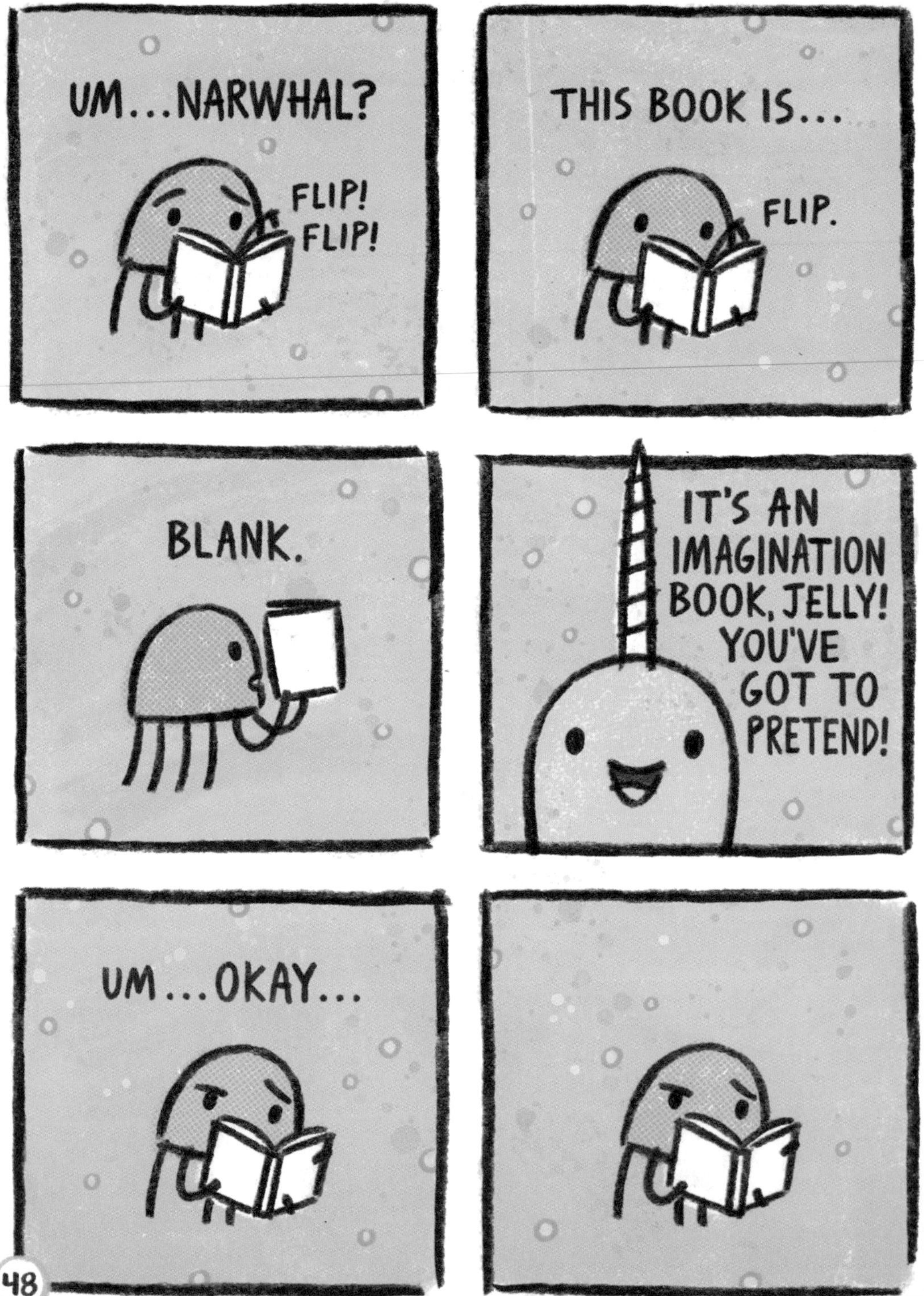
UM...NARWHAL?
FLIP! FLIP!
THIS BOOK IS...
FLIP.
BLANK.
IT'S AN IMAGINATION BOOK, JELLY! YOU'VE GOT TO PRETEND!
UM...OKAY...

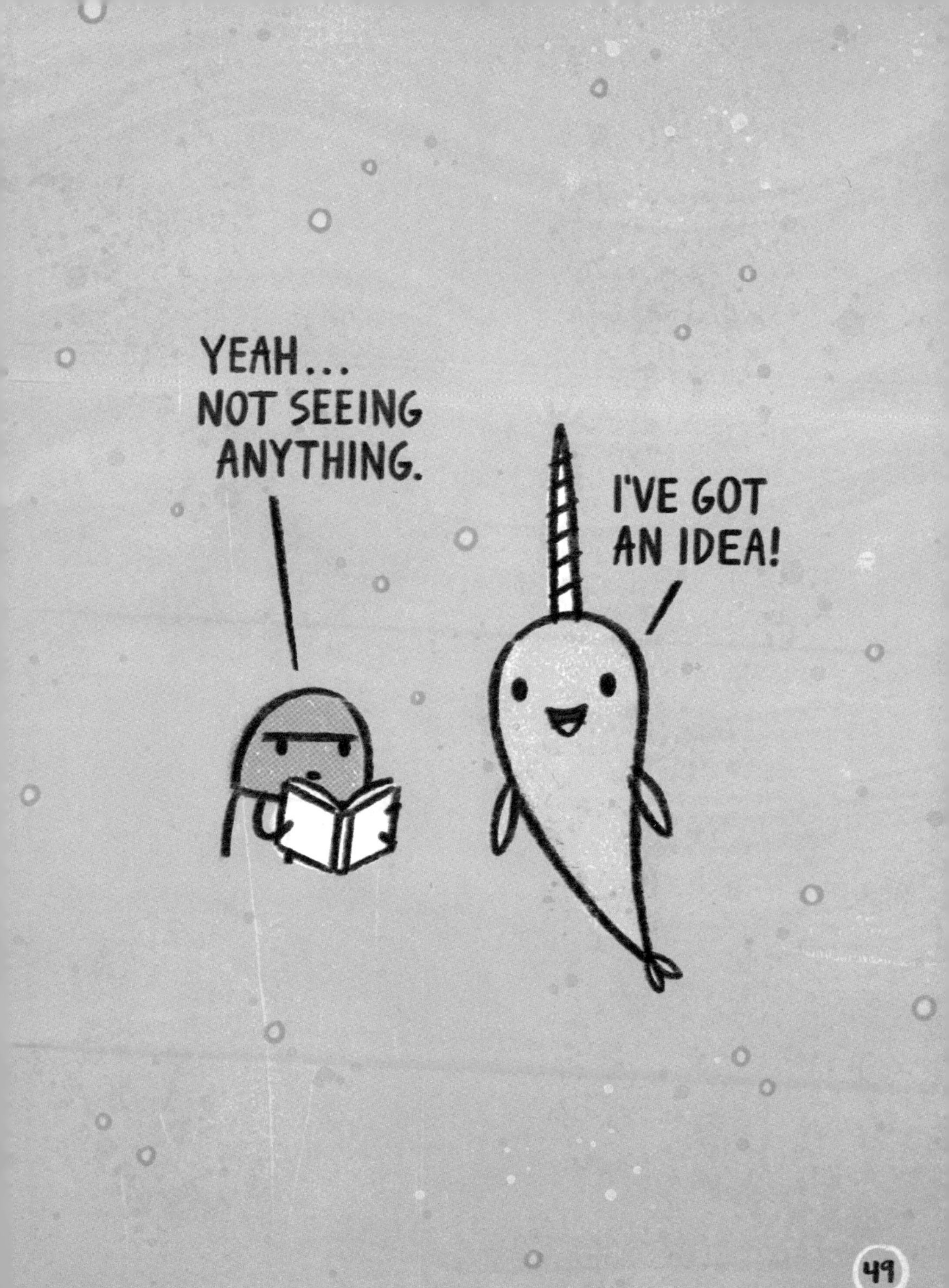
YEAH... NOT SEEING ANYTHING.
I'VE GOT AN IDEA!

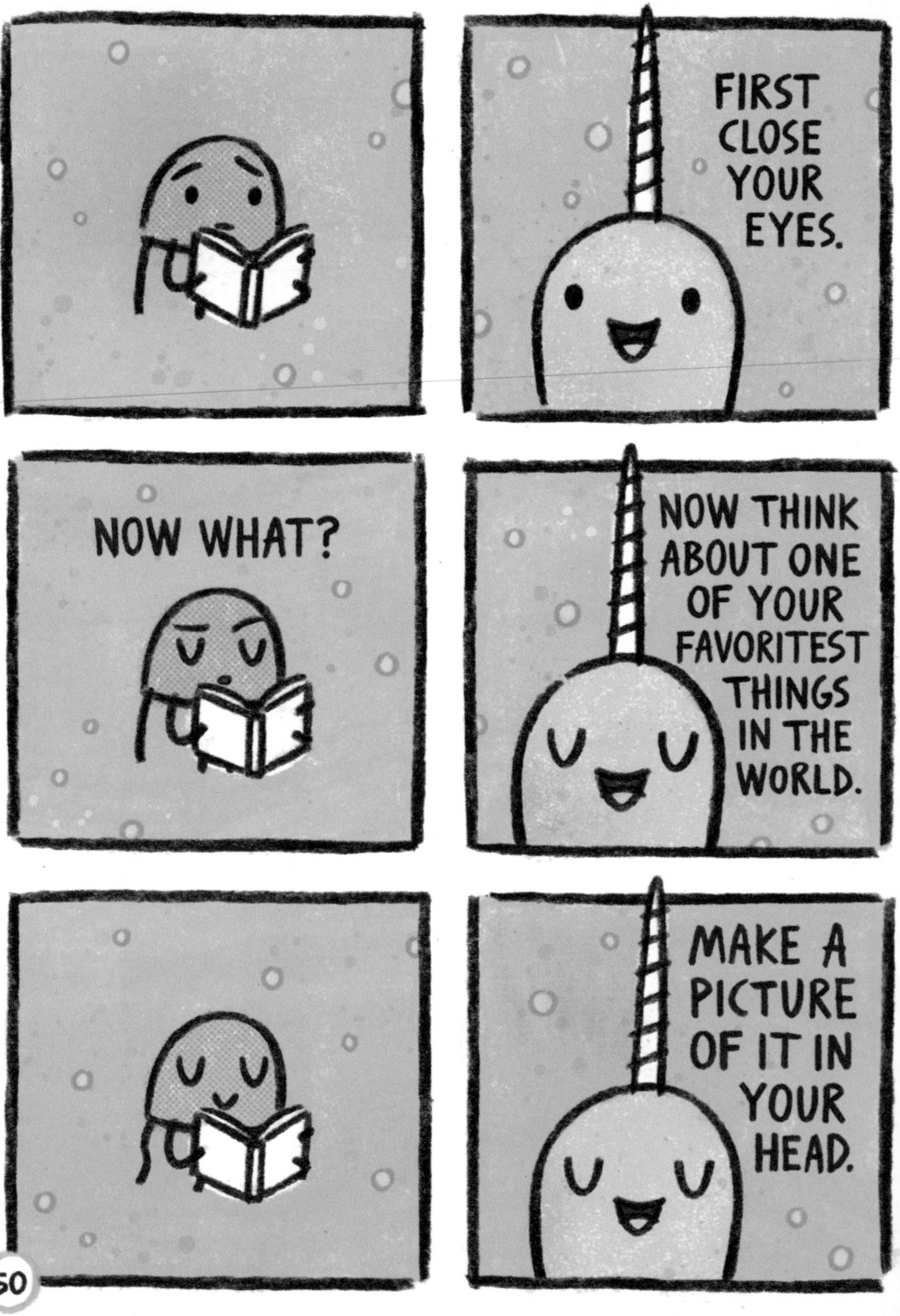
FIRST CLOSE YOUR EYES.
NOW WHAT?
NOW THINK ABOUT ONE OF YOUR FAVORITEST THINGS IN THE WORLD.
MAKE A PICTURE OF IT IN YOUR HEAD.

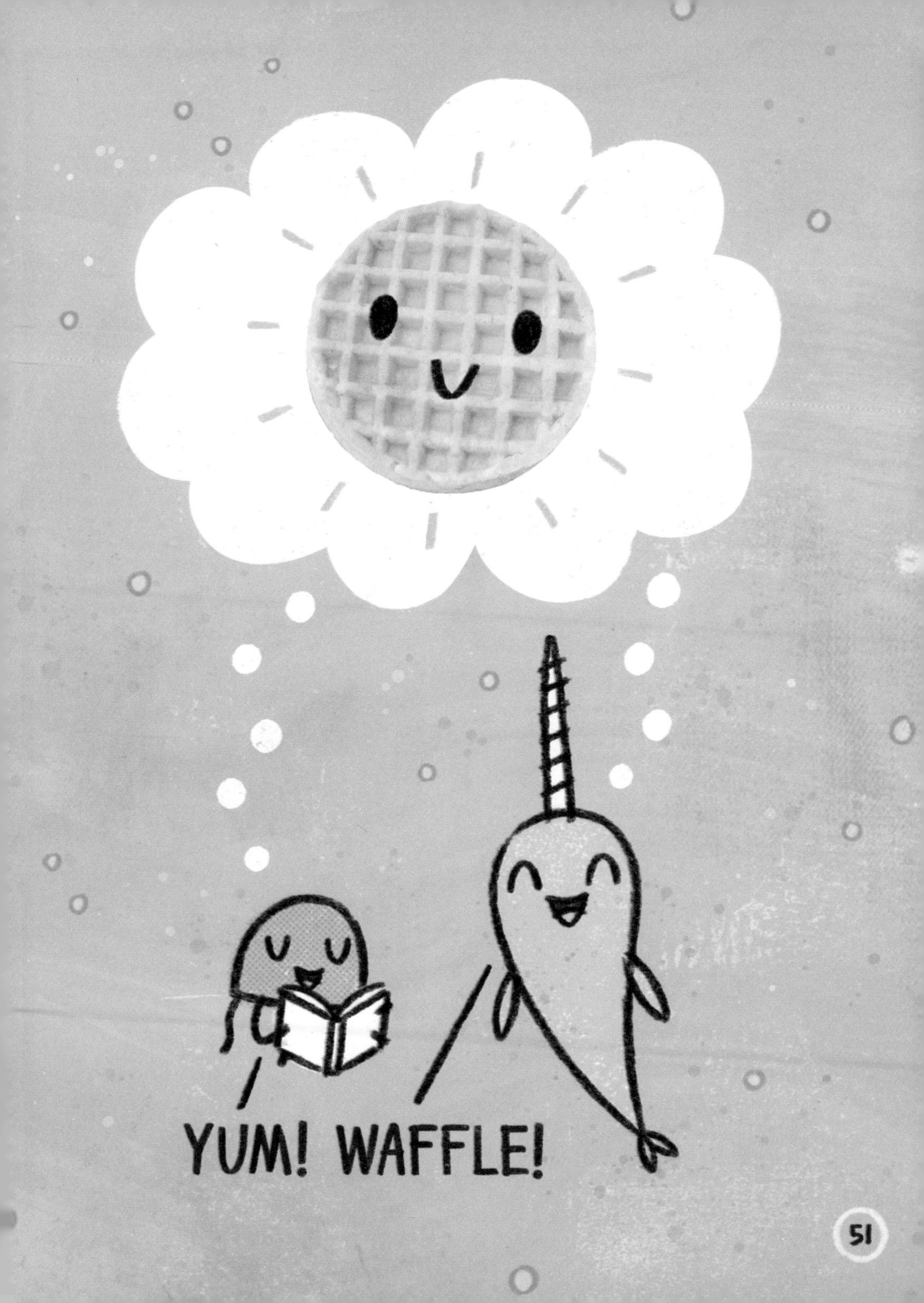
YUM! WAFFLE!

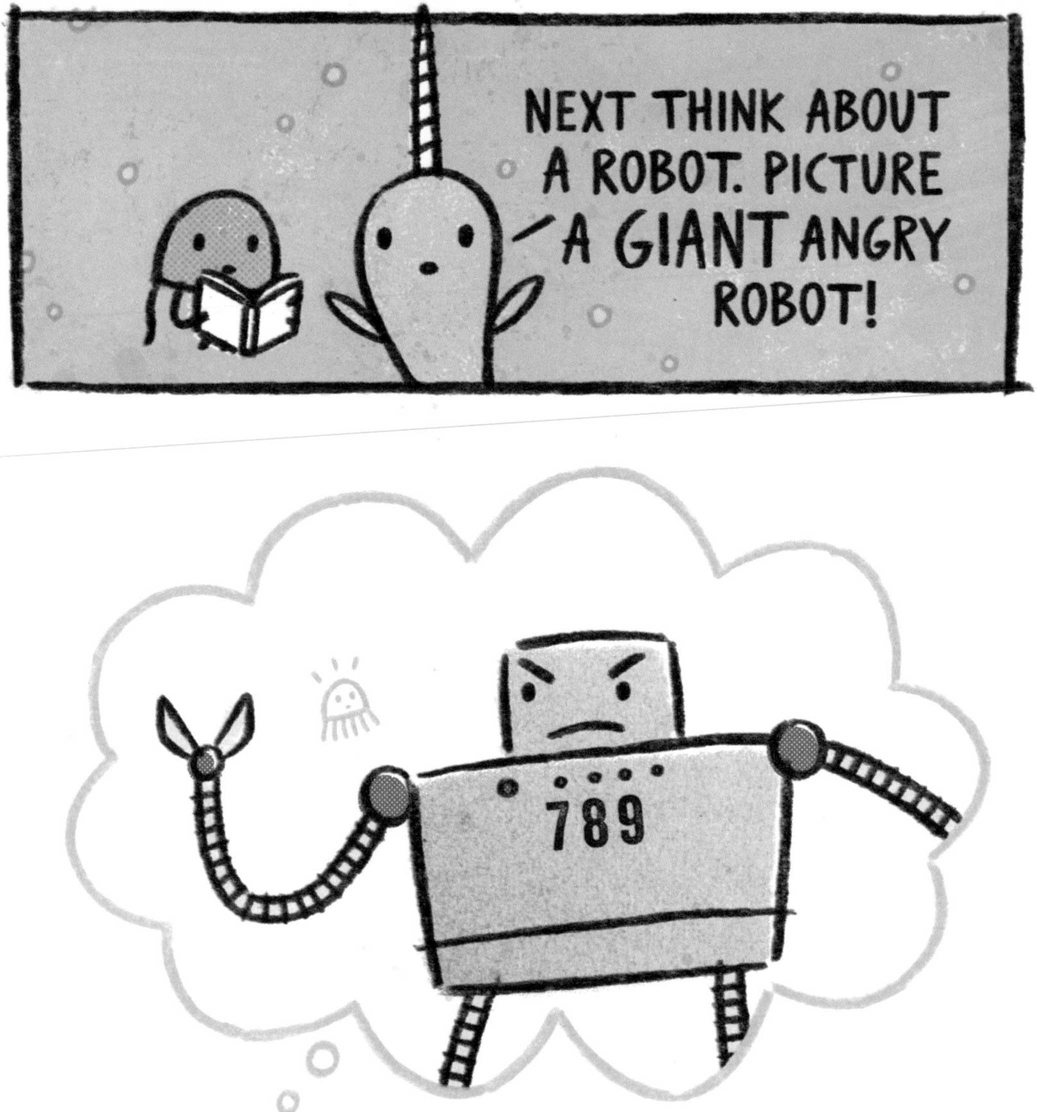
NEXT THINK ABOUT A ROBOT. PICTURE A GIANT ANGRY ROBOT!
789
I'M SCARED OF GIANT ANGRY ROBOTS!

GOOD THING THAT WAFFLE
IS A KUNG FU MASTER!

LOOK AT THE BOOK AND SEE
A PICTURE OF IT BATTLING
THE ROBOT!

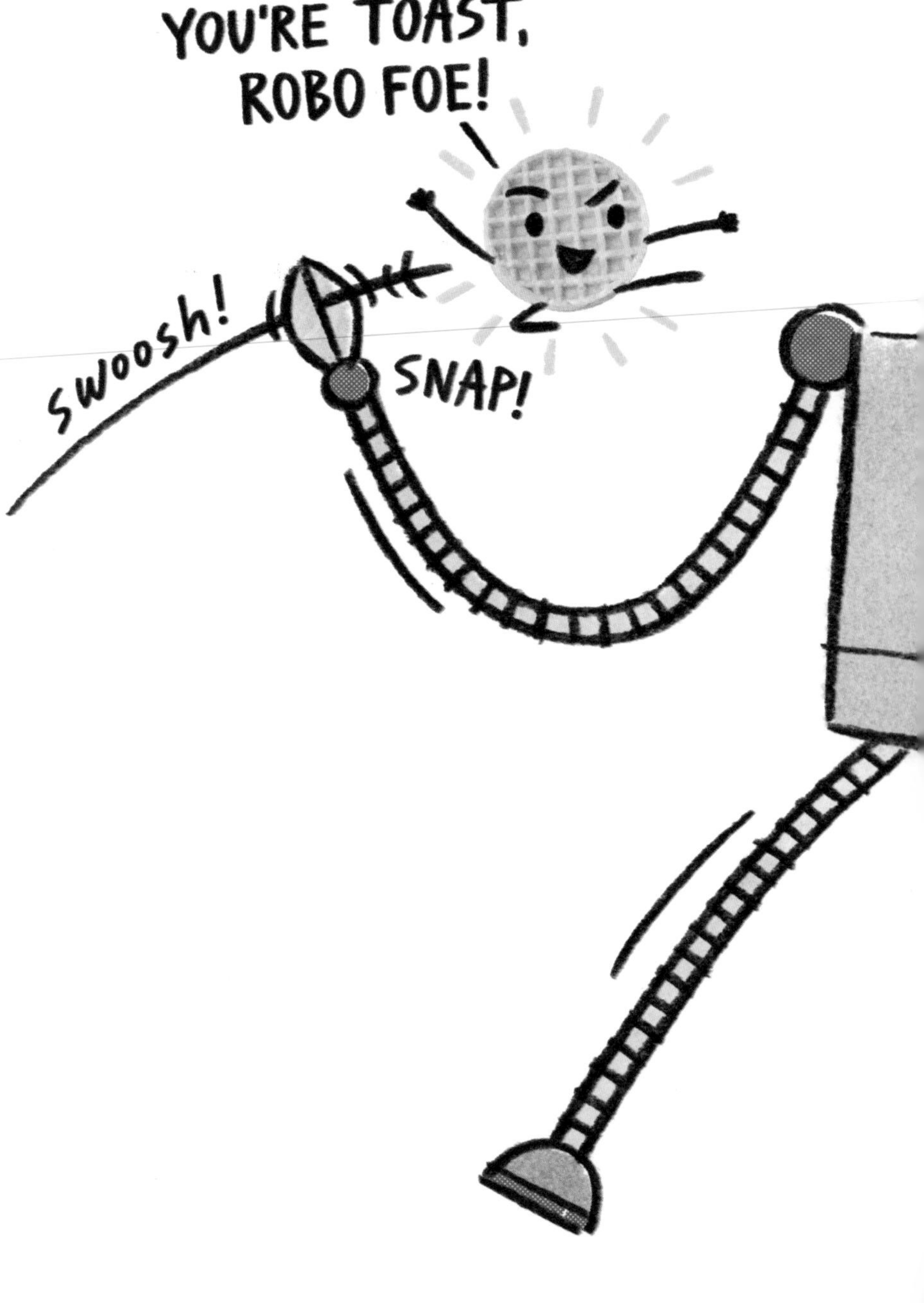
YOU'RE TOAST, ROBO FOE!
SWOOSH!
SNAP!

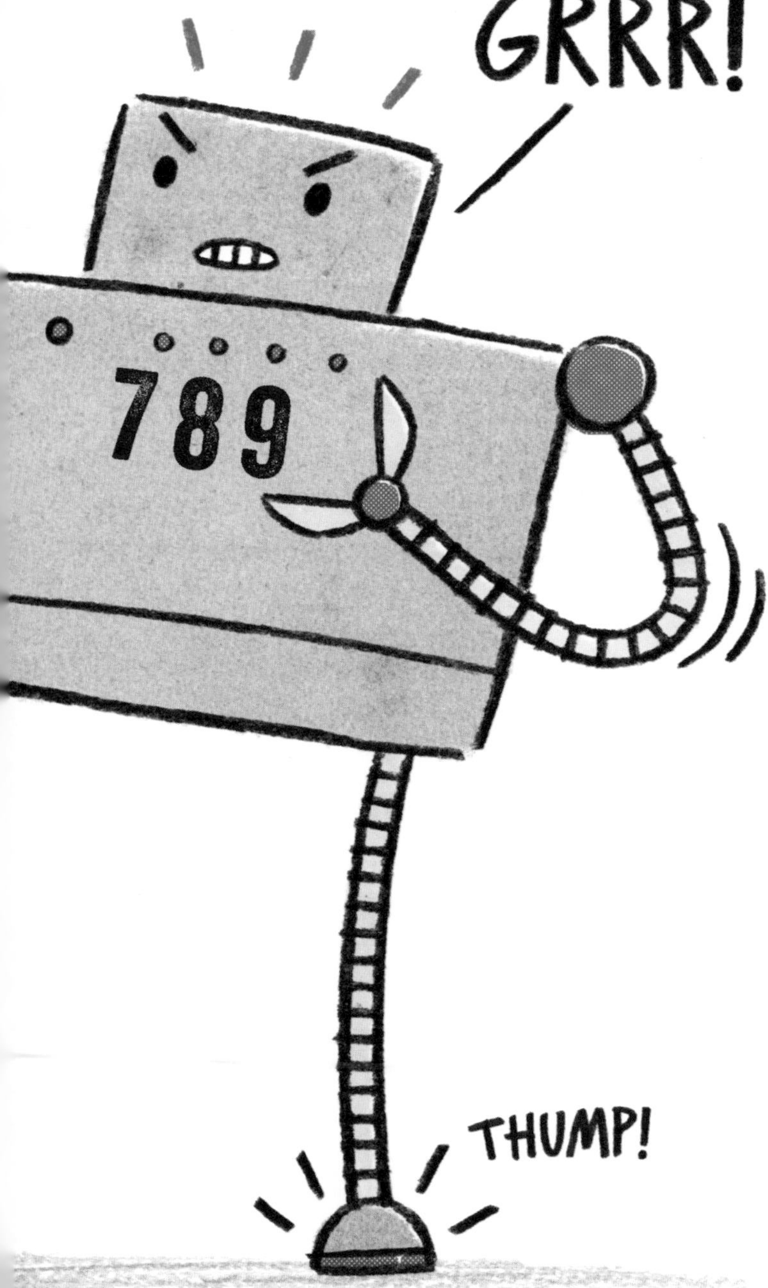
GRRR!
789
THUMP!

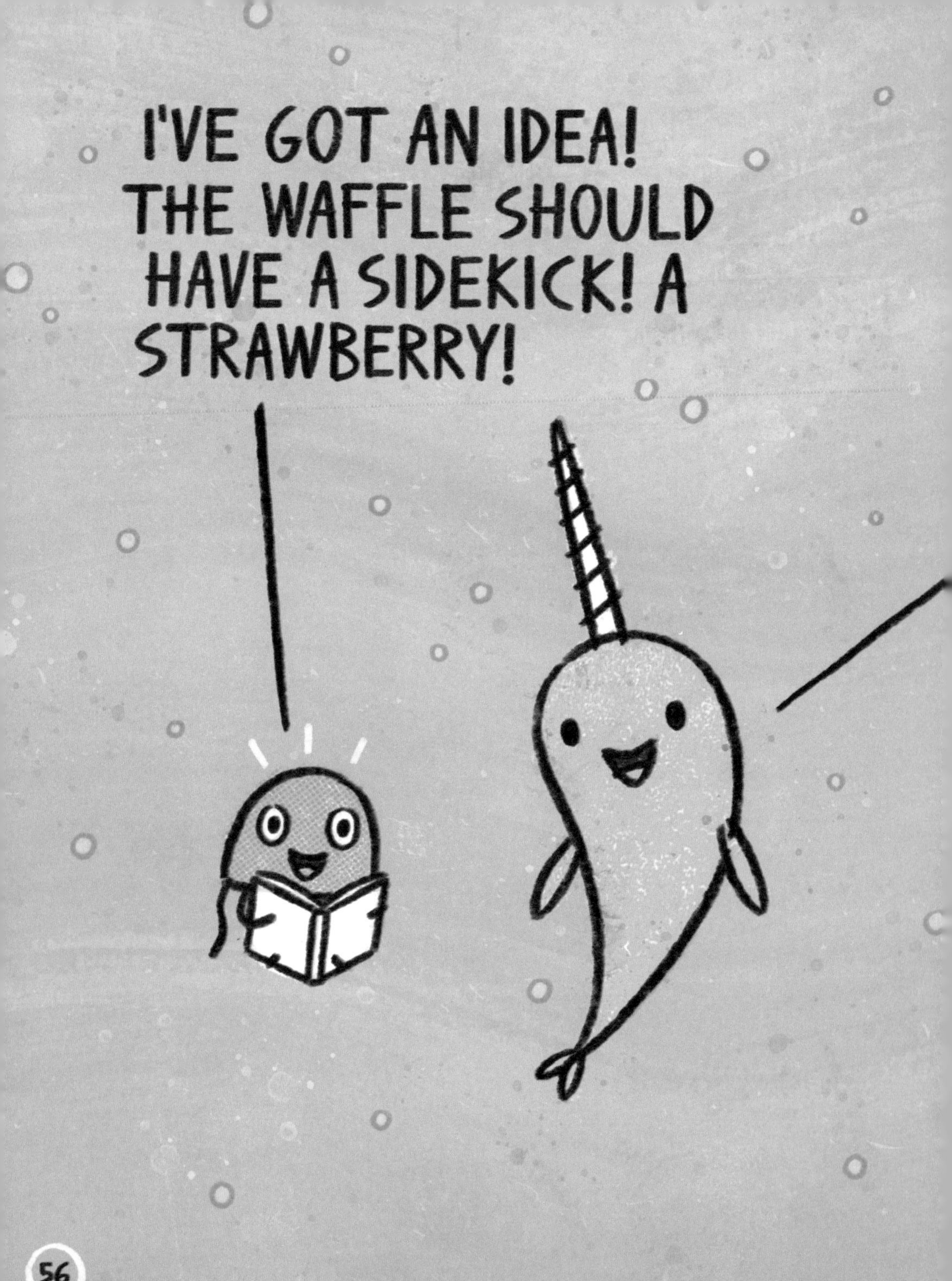
I'VE GOT AN IDEA! THE WAFFLE SHOULD HAVE A SIDEKICK! A STRAWBERRY!

NICE ONE, JELLY!

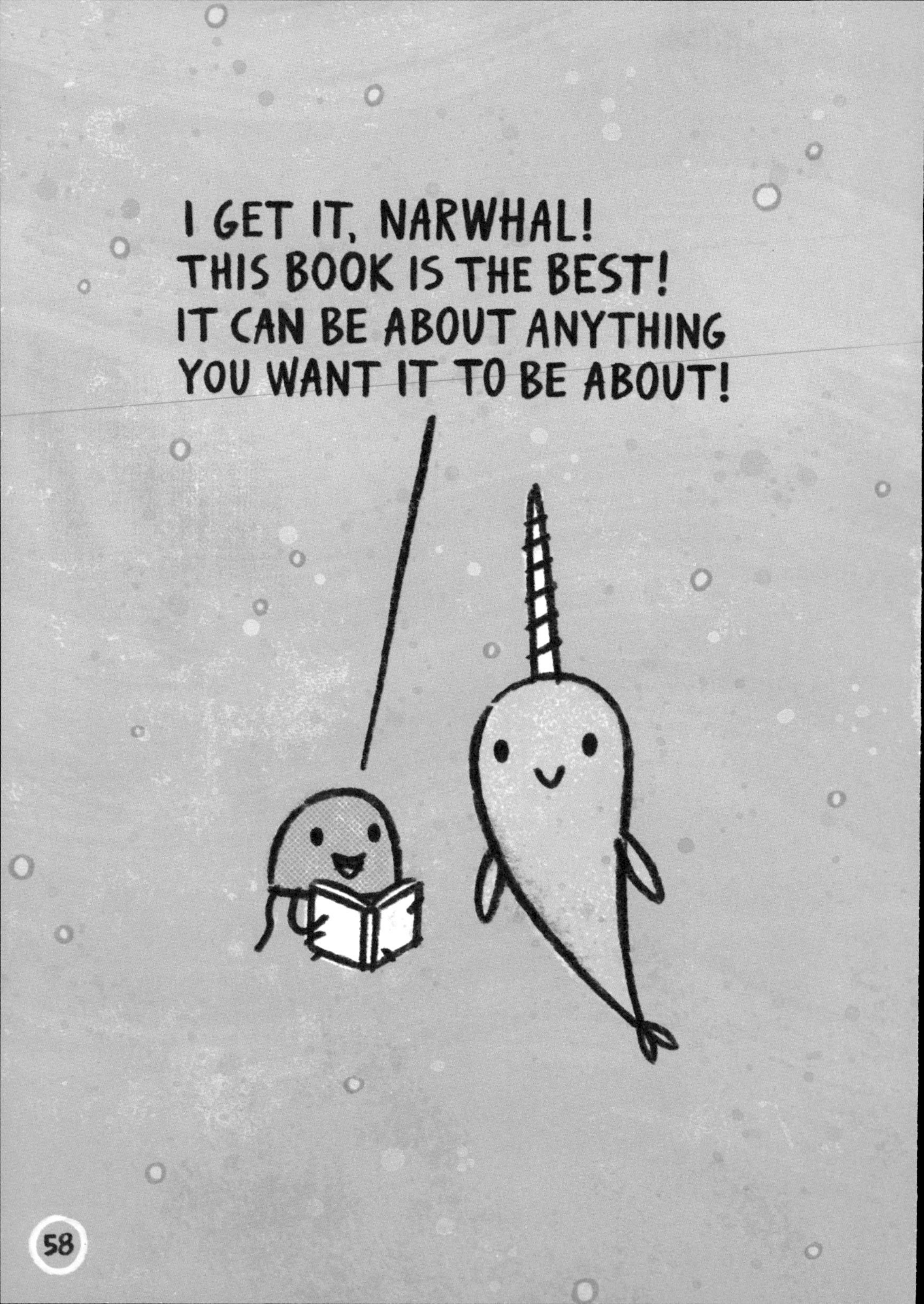
I GET IT, NARWHAL! THIS BOOK IS THE BEST! IT CAN BE ABOUT ANYTHING YOU WANT IT TO BE ABOUT!

TURN THE PAGE!
I WANT TO SEE
WHAT HAPPENS NEXT.

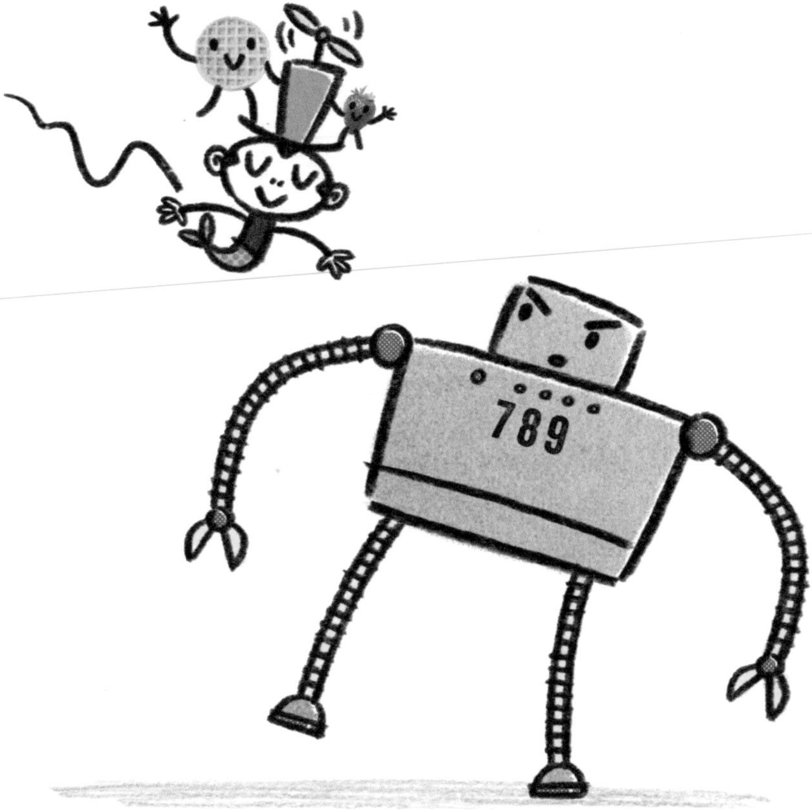
789

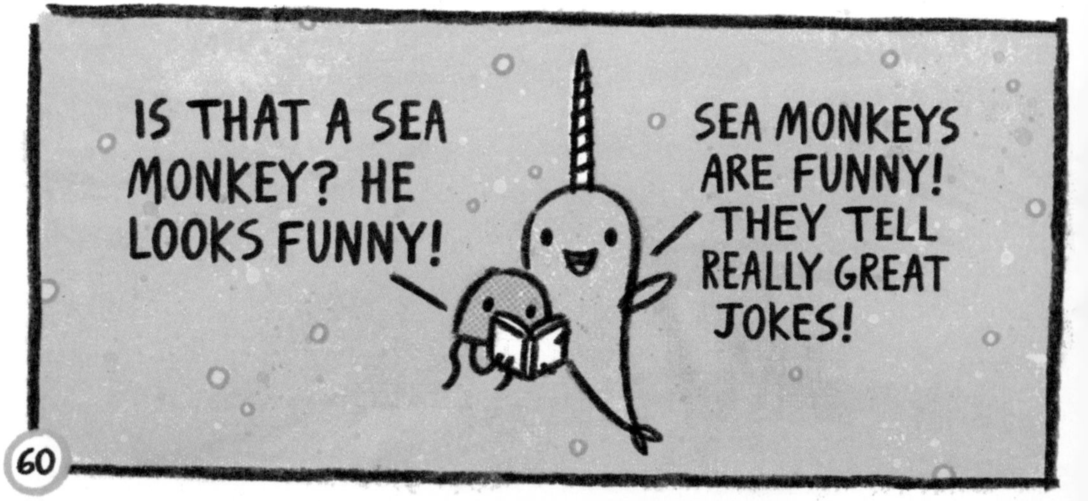
IS THAT A SEA MONKEY? HE LOOKS FUNNY!
SEA MONKEYS ARE FUNNY! THEY TELL REALLY GREAT JOKES!

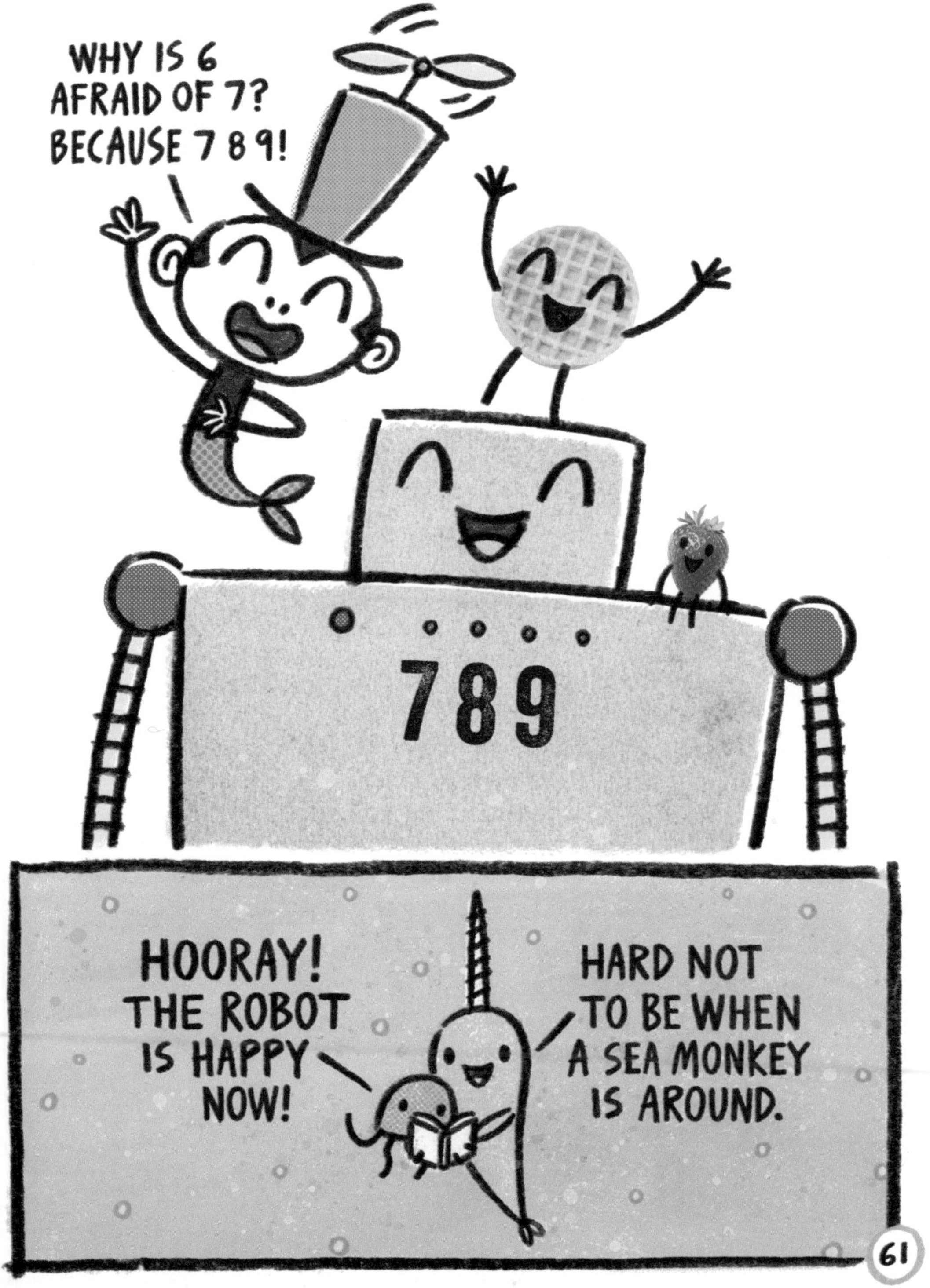
WHY IS 6 AFRAID OF 7? BECAUSE 7 8 9!
789
HOORAY! THE ROBOT IS HAPPY NOW!
HARD NOT TO BE WHEN A SEA MONKEY IS AROUND.

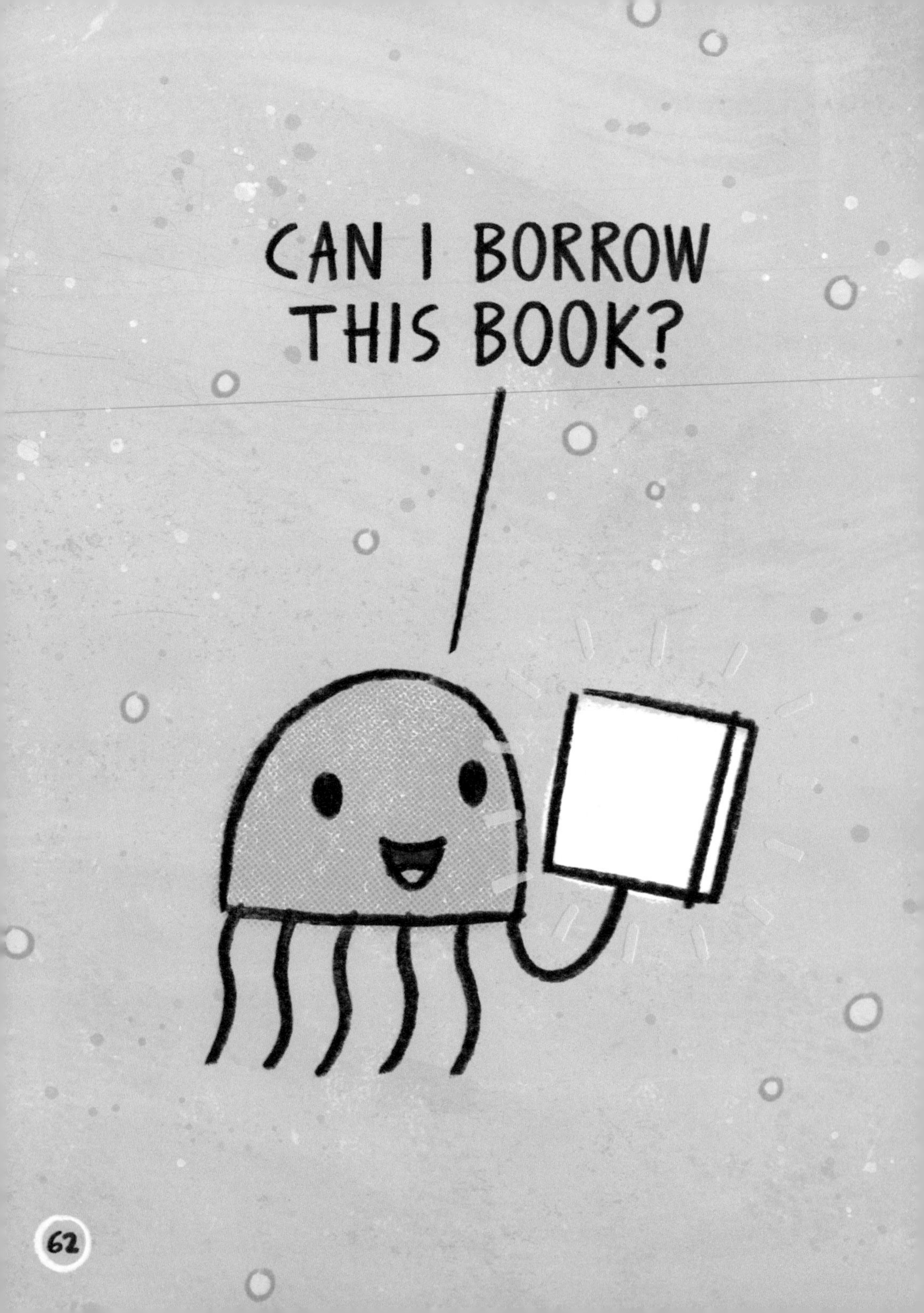
CAN I BORROW THIS BOOK?

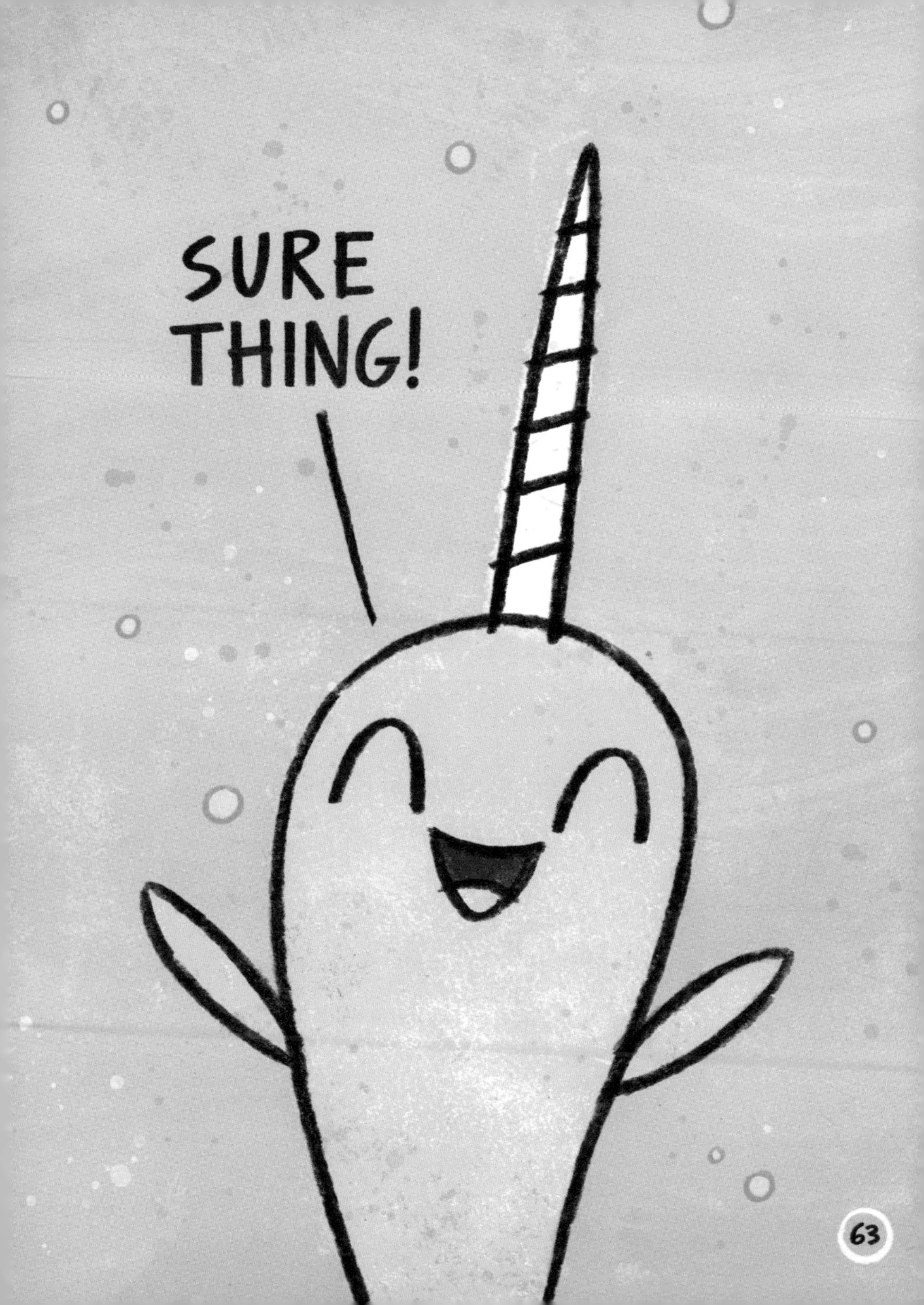
SURE THING!

JUST DON'T GET
THE PAGES WET.

# MORE NARWHAL AND JELLY ADVENTURES COMING SOON!

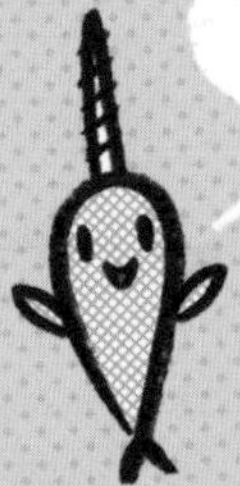

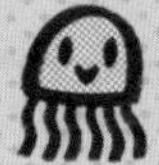

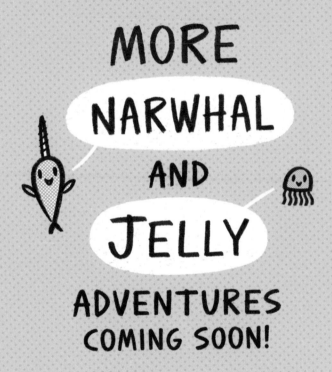

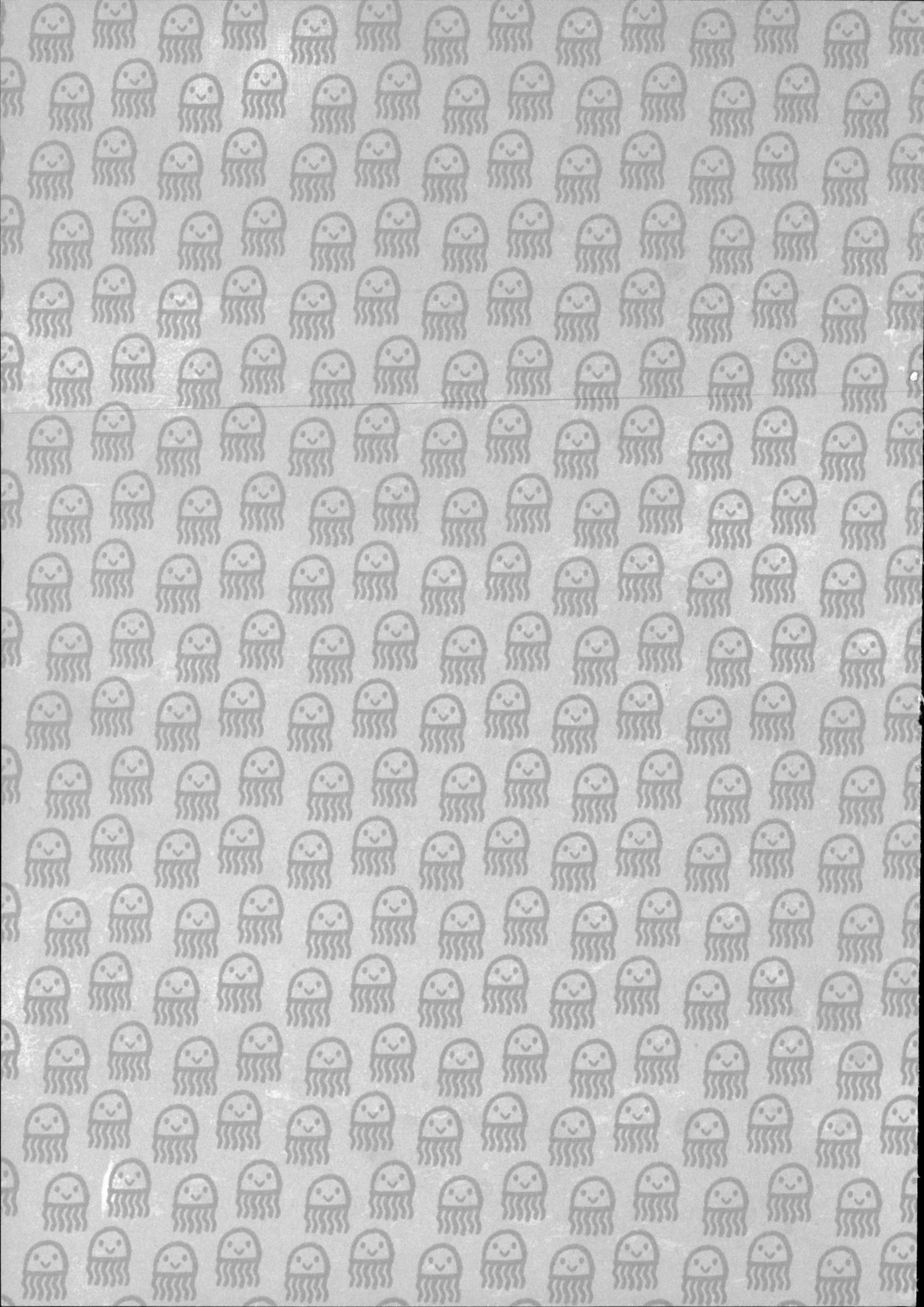